A SCORE WITH A SCOUNDREL

LORDS OF TEMPTATION

TAMMY ANDRESEN

SWIFT ROMANCE PUBLISHING CORP

Keep up with all the latest news, sales, freebies, and releases by joining my newsletter!

www.tammyandresen.com

Hugs!

A SCORE WITH A SCOUNDREL

He's the most enticing rake...

Miss Emma Blake knows she ought not to tangle with Lord Triston Smith. From his bulging muscles to his fierce scowl, every other woman would likely have the sense to stay away from the sort of man who's chosen boxing as his trade. But Emma's never had much smarts when it comes to avoiding problems. Her heart has always been stronger than her brain. And from the moment their eyes meet, she knows he's just the sort of dangerous that might make a woman's bones melt.

And the fact that her mother wishes her to marry the loathsome Lord Marsden only makes Lord Triston that much more interesting. Too bad he finds her more annoying every time they meet. Because he makes her wonder...

Does he have the sort of strength that could save a woman from fate and family?

CHAPTER ONE

Miss Emma Blake tapped her toe beneath her skirts as she and her mother greeted an endless line of guests.

The autumn soirée was an event her family held every year, and her mother had determined that they'd do so again despite the less-than-ideal circumstances. Emma had more or less agreed, though now that she was here, she found she could not decide if she wished to race recklessly from this receiving line and into the ballroom where the lively strains of music had already begun, or if she wanted to run up to her room and hide beneath the covers of her bed.

Every detail appeared the same as previous soirées, with red and gold garland and wreaths adorning every mantel, doorway, and chandelier. Candles filled the entry, hall, and ballroom and a ten-piece orchestra was stationed at one end. But this year was not the same.

Not at all. And not ever again.

Because next to her mother, where her father should have stood, was a blank space.

"Keep your smile firmly in place," her mother whispered from her spot next to Emma. "You must appear the perfect hostess."

Perfect. The word had been bandied about so often of late, Emma wondered if it had lost its meaning. No one was perfect.

Least of all her. But suddenly the expectation was there. A perfect lady would marry the best lord. That was what her mother repeated over and over until Emma wished to go mad from the repetition. Granted, she was considered attractive by many. She was tall, curvy, with striking auburn hair and green eyes. But she was far from a successful debutante. Her season in London had been going well enough, until her father's illness had cut it short. Though she was not as demure as many would like, the gentlemen, at least, had seemed to like her bolder, lively nature. Her mother, however, swore regularly that very trait would lead to her ruin.

Emma's uncle appeared, Emma's younger sister, Natalie, on his arm, and she gave herself a bit of a shake as she watched them approach. Her uncle looked so much like her father that Emma ached a bit every time she shared his company. She and her father had always been close. Where Emma and her mother so often disagreed, her father had simply loved his daughter for who she was without constantly demanding she change. She missed him so much, the pain of his loss sometimes threatened to engulf her.

Her uncle had become the new Viscount Northville, but he'd been kind enough to leave the three women in their home while they first grieved and then decided upon their futures.

Though the only decision left seemed to be whom Emma would marry. Her mother had some inheritance, much of her dowry remained, and her father had left a small property for his wife, but it was, in every way, far less grand than the ancestral home of the Viscount Northville. Which meant that it was left to Emma to marry well and keep her family in the life to which they'd become accustomed.

Emma shook her head. No one had asked her if she wished to marry, or under what circumstances matrimony might suit her. No one seemed to care that a large home was not important to her at all.

What she wanted was some measure of freedom to choose her own future, or even just her own groom. She wished for the ability to find herself and a future that made her feel satisfied rather than forever restless. She was certain a husband of someone else's choosing would give her the opposite experience.

Her mother gave a glittering smile to the Earl of Berwick and his son, the Viscount Marsden, the next guests in line. "So wonderful to see you both," her mother laughed, the tinkling sound ringing out like a bell. "It's been ages." Then she waved airily toward Emma. "You remember my daughter, Miss Emma Blake."

Berwick leaned in to take her mother's hands in his, raising one to his lips, and his son stopped in front of her, giving a short bow. "Lady Emma. You've grown up since last I saw you." His gaze raked over her in a way that made her wildly uncomfortable.

"And you, my lord, look exactly the same." It wasn't exactly true. Was he ten years her senior? He'd filled out a great deal, mostly in the middle, and his hair had thinned considerably. Still, he wasn't entirely unfortunate to look upon and he would be an earl. Her mother would surely consider him an excellent catch.

She caught her mother's approving look out of the corner of her eye as Marsden leaned forward to whisper into her ear. "You must save me a dance."

She gave a nod of acceptance and he moved closer still. Emma resisted the urge to step back, realizing that she'd answered her earlier question about which way she'd like to run. She no longer had any desire go into the ballroom—she now wished to go directly to her room.

But she kept her feet planted and the father and son moved on, making way for the next guests.

She didn't look at them, her eyelids had fluttered closed as she attempted to calm the beat of her heart, the desire to run. She'd like to be on her horse, riding over the open fields. Or perhaps in London, blending into the sea of people. Anywhere but here.

"Why hello," her mother gushed from next to her. "Such a pleasure to finally meet you."

Emma's eyes snapped back open, her breath catching as her gaze collided with another's.

Lord Triston Smith. Her heartbeat ticked back up, pounding in her chest, as his dark eyes held hers captive. Near black in color, they were fringed with long lashes, which managed to draw even more attention to his glittering gaze. Those lashes were the only soft thing about him. That and his dark, wavy hair.

Every other part of him was hard, from his jaw to the chiseled cut of his shoulders, right down to his powerful thighs on full display in the tight breeches he wore.

His mouth was set in a perpetually hard frown, at least that was her impression. This was only the second time she'd met him, the first encounter being very brief, but his mouth appeared natural in the stern expression—which should likely have frightened her.

Somehow, it wasn't fear but sizzling awareness and a keen interest that coursed through her once again. Why had the handful of words they'd exchanged been as gruff as his stern frown? Was there any soft-ness underneath that hard exterior?

She shivered, not with fear but with interest as his brother, Lord Smith, took her mother's offered hand.

His wife came next. Lady Smith was as sweet as her looks implied. During their one meeting, the beautiful blonde had been warm and generous with her time and her compliments.

Emma had instantly liked her.

"Lady Emma," Lady Smith gave her a large smile. "So good to see you again. Thank you for having us."

"I'm so glad you've come." Those felt like the first genuine words she'd said all evening. And something inside her uncoiled, her entire body relaxing. "I've been hoping to visit you again, but we've been so busy with preparations."

Lady Smith waved her hand. "I understand. Perhaps next week we could have tea."

"I'd like that very much," she answered, watching Lord Triston greet her mother.

He bowed, that stiff frown still marking his face, hardly uttering a word beyond a gruff, "Good evening."

Even her mother eyed him with a bit of skepticism as she replied. "Good evening."

Lord Triston was the exact sort of man her mother would despise. And not just because he was rougher in every way from a normal lord. He was a third son, unlikely to ever gain a title. That was his worst sin of all.

Emma attempted to care. She really did. She knew how important a good marriage was to her mother, to her family. But as she looked into those dark eyes, excitement settled deep in the pit of her stomach.

"Lord Triston," Emma supplied with a shaking breath. "A pleasure to see you again."

And she meant those words. Far more than she ought.

———

TRIS GROANED to himself as he stared into the green eyes that he was certain belonged to the devil.

Oh, Lady Emma looked innocent enough.

Auburn hair and ivory skin. Full, lush pink lips that always had a ready smile. And he wouldn't even start on her figure. Because that was where the devilment began. Her curves were made for sin.

And the look in her eyes…oh, they were the color of grass after a spring rain and the tiny yellow flecks appeared like sunshine itself, but beneath that…they held the glint of trouble.

He'd recognize the look anywhere.

He was one of five brothers who'd grown up as the bastard sons of the Earl of Easton. Through a stroke of fate, and the helping hand of their one legitimate sibling, they had been legitimatized, but they'd been raised on the East End of London. And one learned to spot bad intentions with a single glance, and this lady may as well have been holding up a sign.

Is she did, it would read:

I'LL RUIN your life if you let me.

. . .

AND HE HAD no intention of allowing a woman to disrupt his path. Though a lord now, Tris had never actually expected to be so. After spending much of his childhood thieving, fighting, and generally causing mayhem, he'd settled into the sport of boxing as a way to channel his feelings and his need for chaos.

The anger that had plagued him still simmered underneath the surface. He'd just learned to focus those feelings into his training and into his fights, fairly certain he was too explosive for *any* woman.

And he knew without a doubt that a woman like Lady Emma was as far away as the moon.

He saw the interest shining in her eyes. He'd seen it before. Ladies liked his strength, they found his hard edges intriguing, until they brushed against one.

Once she was married, she might invite him into her bed for a torrid affair and he'd likely accept. The attraction he felt for her was near explosive, so deep, it was a well that would surely drown him.

But as a debutante, she was someone he'd best stay as far away from as possible. He had his own goals and ambitions with his career, and dallying with a daughter of a powerful family was the surest way to see them crushed.

Which was why, when he stopped in front of her, he looked over her left shoulder, not meeting her gaze, as he murmured, "Lady Emma."

"My lord," she replied, her breath catching on the second word. Despite his best efforts, he tensed at the breathiness he heard. Her obvious interest.

He willed himself back to calm, knowing that here, of all places, he could not lose control of himself. He already stuck out at this ball, or party, or whatever the hell they'd called the bloody affair.

Taller, larger than every man here, and far more muscled, he barely fit into his coat. The rest of these titled gentlemen had a softness about them. Easy lives, good food. He bet none of them had ever brawled in the streets or had knife fights with boys twice their size. They'd never fought to feed their baby sisters or thieved for the same reason.

Tris had always been filled with raw aggression and it didn't fit in this clean and beautiful world. He looked about the entry with its soaring ceilings and intricate plaster. The polish of the carved banister shone in the candlelight as guests made their way up the curved stairs to the ballroom.

"Thank you for coming," Emma continued, leaning forward in a way that better displayed her cleavage. He couldn't help himself. He looked down at the plump, round, smooth flesh.

His cock gave a definite twitch and he forced himself not to notice how her bosom was precisely the perfect size. Not overmuch, it was just enough, assuring him that her breasts would fill a man's hands. He tried to tear his gaze away but failed miserably.

Nor could he help but trace the narrow curve of her waist or the flare of her hips with his gaze. He'd bet her ass was nice and plump and round.

He clenched both fists at his sides. "The pleasure is mine." The words sat bitter on his tongue. It was not a pleasure but a torture.

"Will you be staying at Upton Falls for long?"

The answer was that he didn't know. The family ran a gaming hell, Hell's Corner. When a competitor had threatened his brother's wife, Tris had agreed to come here to ensure her safety.

But damned if he was telling this woman any of that. He knew she only asked because she was making plans... What sort he couldn't say. But whatever they were, he wanted no part of them. "Not long."

She gave him an overly bright smile that told him of her disappointment. For his part, he'd stay at this particular party for as short a time as possible and then he'd slip away. The Northville estate was the neighboring property to his brother's. He could walk back at any point. In fact, the night air would likely help cool his overheated skin.

Saying a curt goodbye, he followed his brother Rush and Rush's wife, Abby, up the grand stairs and into the ballroom, his teeth grinding together as he noted the marble floors that gleamed under his feet.

Next to him, some woman with plumes of feathers sticking out her headdress gave an overly enthusiastic giggle. "I just love the Northville soirée. What shall we do when they no longer host it?"

A sneer pulled at his lip. The carpets were thick and lush, a red that only accented the decorations for the soirée. Christ, even that word spoke of snobbery.

Soirée.

Soirée.

It sounded odder each time he repeated it. Utter shit. A sea of sparkling women passed him, all in jewels that caught the candlelight and twinkled as their wearer moved.

One of those stones could have fed an entire tenement house where he came from. Where people were packed in like fish in a barrel and still starving.

He tugged on the lapels of his jacket. What was he even doing here?

He'd wanted no part of this life. He'd keep his brother safe. And Abby too. The woman was as sweet as they came, but he'd never wished to attend a soirée.

He already had a profession as a boxer and that suited him perfectly well. The only reason he'd agreed to help his family with the club was that he wanted to take his career further.

At nearly thirty, he was growing too old for the ring. It had occurred to him that he might start a boxing club of his own. He could train and spar and use the club as the release of pressure without so much risk to his personal health.

Which was why he'd entered the gaming business with his brothers. Because while it created one headache after another, it also afforded him enough income that he'd nearly saved all that he needed for the purchase of his own club.

And leaving to help Rush in the country would only prove to his brothers that they could run the business without him.

A good plan, if he did say so himself, except for this one complication. He'd landed himself at a bloody soirée.

Stationing himself against a wall, he leaned back, crossing his ankles and his arms in an attempt to make himself as unappealing as possible.

It didn't work. Woman after woman eyed him over her fan, their eyes filled with interest or suggestion—or both.

He ignored any implied invitations.

A few years back, he'd dallied with a countess. When her husband had found out, Triston nearly landed in the Tower. He'd only avoided it by hopping on a ship with his brother Fulton and spending three months in Italy while his brother smuggled wine.

He'd not make such a mistake again.

Besides, any desire he might feel for these women was dulled by his dislike for their vapid self-regard.

Lady Emma entered the ballroom, her hand tucked into some man's arm. She laughed as he spoke, her smile so large, it looked brittle.

The man who escorted her was the exact sort that Tris despised. Soft. That was the word for it.

With a growl of disgust, he pushed off the wall and went in search of Rush. He was leaving. His brother could spend as long as he wished here, but Tris had had enough.

CHAPTER TWO

EMMA WATCHED Lord Triston push off the wall and stalk across the ballroom. There was no other word for the way he moved. He was at least a head taller than every other man and certainly every woman, and the crowd parted for him, allowing him to move freely.

For the briefest moment, she thought he might be coming toward her. Did he wish to speak with her again? Did he feel the same tug toward her that she did him?

But he veered around her and Lord Marsden, moving toward the door.

Her mouth turned down, disappointment making her shoulders slump.

"What is wrong, my lady?" Marsden asked, pulling her closer.

She ignored the need to put distance between them as she pasted another smile on her face. She attempted to employ all the charm her mother had taught her. "Nothing, my lord, though I greatly appreciate you asking."

He searched her face, the light in his eyes nearly making her wince away. But he didn't seem to notice as he pressed. "Surely it is something."

Did she answer? Clearly, she shouldn't tell him of her disappointment over Lord Smith. But that didn't mean she couldn't be honest. "I must confess I am struggling this evening. This was always an event over which my father presided."

His hand came to her back, rubbing a small circle just above her derriere. The boldness of his touch surprised her, and she froze. No man touched a woman he wasn't married to in such a way. But she attempted to relax. The gesture was likely meant as a comfort, but from him...

Marsden didn't seem to notice as he pulled her toward the open doors that lined the ballroom's far wall. They opened onto a series of balconies that overlooked the grounds. "What you need is some air."

That sounded lovely. The noise was already making her head ache, her temples throbbing every time she pulled her smile wider.

Lord Marsden led her outside, the cool night air fanning her skin, some of the tension uncoiling in her muscles.

What she needed was a chance to escape. Leave the home where every room reminded her of her father, leave her mother's constant pressure, leave the fate that loomed over her.

They stepped out onto the balcony, and she let out a long sigh of relief. "Oh. This is much better. Thank you, Lord Marsden."

"You're most welcome," he answered quietly from just behind her.

Emma attempted to ignore his company as her eyes had fluttered closed and she allowed the breeze to cool her skin, the artful pieces that had been left loose from her coiffure moving against her face. "My mother wished to have this party to help me, but I'm not certain—"

"And what does she think you need help with?" There was an intensity to his voice that startled her, and the muscles that had loosened since stepping out onto the balcony tightened again.

She took a small step to the left, wanting more distance between them before she turned to look at him. Her instinct had been correct. He was far closer than she'd imagined. "The season will be coming soon and..."

"I heard you had a very good showing during your first season. That is to say, before you returned here for your father's health."

"I did, I think." She shrugged, eyeing him as she took another casual step back. He unnerved her. It was his stance or his eyes, but the hair on the back of her neck had risen and she felt the need to escape.

He took a definite step forward, closing the distance between them. "In what ways did you struggle?"

She drew in a breath, trying to decide how one answered that question. Especially when they hardly knew one another. "All the ways someone who is new to something might."

"Really?" he asked, his voice dropping as his gaze raked down her body. She shrank back, being careful to move toward the door rather than past it into the dark corner of the balcony. There, they'd be out of sight of the crowd. "I heard you specifically struggled with brashness."

Her mouth dropped open as she forgot her retreat. "I beg your pardon?"

One of his brows quirked. "Don't look offended, my lady. I wish to be open with you."

His idea of open seemed to be that he could insult her without repercussion. "Am I to be open with you as well?"

"Tut tut," he whispered with a smile. "This is what they were talking about, weren't they? You're a fighter."

Her mouth clamped shut as she took another step back. One more and she'd be in the doorway between the balcony and the ballroom, which was, in her estimation, a far safer place to be. "And you are too forward."

He laughed then, low and a bit menacing. "Would you think me so if I told you that I am considering you for my future countess? Lovely as you are, I must confess that I like a bit of spirit."

Her mouth opened to tell him that he might consider her all he wished but she did not intend to indulge him. She'd starve on the streets of London before she allowed an arrogant man like this to make her his prisoner.

But she never got the words out.

His arm reached out, pulling her with such a quick jerk she nearly lost her footing. As she attempted to right herself, he spun her into the shadows. He might have been softer than she liked, but he was strong enough to overpower her.

He pinned her between the railing and his own body, his stomach pressing into hers. "My lord," she gasped, as her gaze flew to his. "Unhand me."

But he only gave her a lecherous grin. "Your mother has already informed my father that a match between our families would be most welcome. Not only will I not unhand you but I'm going to give you the briefest lesson on how a wife submits to her husband."

And then his lips came down on hers.

She attempted to scream then, but could only push the briefest sound out before his lips crashed over her mouth, giving her a punishing kiss that made her cry out. The sound was lost too, muffled by the brutal force of his kiss.

She tried to fight, attempted to push him back, but his hands were like vises around her upper arms.

She'd kissed before. Once. It had been a sweet sigh of a touch that had left her swooning for days.

This was a punishment. How long it would last and to what length it would go, she had no idea. She'd felt perpetually trapped of late but, at this moment, she was at Marsden's complete mercy. How was she to get out of this terrible situation?

———

TRIS WALKED out the front door and then veered right, so that he might cut across the rolling field that spread between the two properties. He skirted the estate toward the back.

Even in the moonlight, he could see the bucolic beauty of this place. Manicured gardens, hemmed by rolling fields and wooded paths. Something in him revolted at the wholesomeness. Even the air was cleaner here.

The only thing dirty was himself. He shook his head, dispelling the thought. The people in there were the filthy ones. They all pretended

TAMMY ANDRESEN

to be better, spent their time in their pretty world, ignoring the evils just beyond their doors.

He wasn't dirtier for living in the filth, they were for pushing all the dirt into piles far beyond their doors.

All the balcony doors were open, allowing the light and music to filter across the lawn. From here, the party looked grand, but he still snorted with disgust.

He could hear the music filtering outside, the rise and fall of their voices like waves rolling on a beach. But he knew the truth. They sounded beautiful from afar, but up close, when he'd be able to hear their individual words, they were a vapid and vain lot full of their own self-worth.

He snorted again, looking back over his shoulder one last time. Never again. He'd come this once with the idea of keeping Abby safe. Perhaps he should have stayed. Would the man who had threatened his family appear here?

He grimaced as he turned back toward the party. Had he allowed his own irritation to cause him to act with poor judgment? He sighed. Why had the sight of Emma on that man's arm riled him so?

But he didn't think on it further, and then he caught sight of a couple on the balcony. The moonlight glinted off her hair and if he wasn't mistaken, it was red.

He narrowed his gaze as he watched her creeping away from the man, who moved closer, looking distinctly like a predator.

The protector in Tris rose to the surface. Why, he couldn't say. Tris often acted on instinct, and he did so now as he moved closer, back toward the house.

The situation was likely none of his business, but he couldn't shake the idea that it was Emma on the balcony. And while she was not his concern—a woman to be avoided—the idea of another man touching her…

He watched as the man grabbed the lady in question, pulling her into the shadows, heard her strangled cry before it was abruptly cut off.

A growl rose in his own throat and he quickened his pace.

Below the balcony was a window with a heavy stone sill. Years of training had made him quick and strong and with hardly a bother, he planted a foot on the sill, pushing himself up into the air where he grabbed an iron spindle next to the man's feet.

He did two hundred pull-ups a day, and he'd just fashioned a bar in Rush's stable to keep up the routine. Hand over hand, he pulled himself up the bars and then grabbed the railing, getting a foot on the balcony in the space between the lower rail and the floor. Quickly, he heaved a foot over and then he was behind the man, the lady's cries muffled by the bastard's mouth.

Tris ought to think for a moment. Who knew for certain what circumstances had brought this couple out here or what was actually happening?

But the woman gave another cry and the part inside him that was a brother, a man of honor, roared to the surface and his hand shot out, wrapping about the back of the man's neck in a vise-like grip that instantly turned the other man to stone.

He yanked him away from the woman with all the power he possessed, the man stumbling, his feet tangling, and then he was falling.

Tris let him go, allowing him to tumble to the floor, hard. A grunting cry erupted when the fellow's shoulder hit the surface.

"Lord Triston?" He turned back, meeting Emma's wide green eyes. So, it *had* been Emma. He'd sensed it was her, which should have frightened him, but he didn't think on it more as he turned, placing himself between Emma and the other man, blocking her with his body.

"How dare you touch me in such a way." The man had the audacity to growl as he attempted to pull himself up from where he'd splatted on the floor.

"He is the Viscount Marsden," Emma whispered, her hand touching his shoulder.

He shrugged, the rank of no consequence to him.

The man rose, the same one he'd seen with Emma earlier. His chest expanded. "Nice to meet you, Marsden."

The man sneered at him. "I'll end you."

Tris snorted. He'd like to see this man try. "Is that with your superior strength or your intellect?"

"I'm the heir to an earldom."

"And I a marquessate." All right. That was likely misleading. Nor did he usually play these rank games. But he hated the pompous arrogance that had nothing to do with a single accomplishment.

Marsden stopped, his lip curling. "This isn't over."

A man only said that when it was, in fact, over. He'd been in hundreds of male competitions in his life and that was the exact phrase every male said when he was conceding. His brows lifted as he shooed the man away like an annoying fly. Then he stopped. "Touch Lady Emma again and I will kill you. Don't think I can't."

"You dare to threaten me?"

Emma's hand flitted down his back, her breath blowing against his neck. "You don't have to..." she whispered.

Didn't she know he'd enjoy it?

"Rejoin the party, Lord Marsden, and have a safe trip home. May we never meet again."

"Oh, we'll meet again," Marsden said, yanking the lapels of his coat and smoothing his hand over his hair before he turned and reentered the ballroom.

Was that supposed to scare Tris?

A muffled sob sounded behind him, and he looked over his shoulder to see Emma with her hand covering her mouth, her green eyes filled with tears.

Christ. He had a soft spot for a teary woman. Two sisters did that to a man.

He found himself turning and pulling her into his arms. "Don't cry." Hadn't he just been lecturing himself to keep as much distance between him and Emma as possible? She was one of them. And he had plans that did not involve a viscount's troublesome daughter. Now here he was hugging her, for pity's sake. Hugging.

"I'm so sorry," she gasped. "He frightened me and..."

She was so damn soft in his arms, her curves molding to him, her cheek resting against his chest. "It's over now."

"My mother wants me to wed that piece of shit."

It was the profanity that had him pulling back to look at her. Not even his sisters, who'd grown up on the East End, used such language.

Heat flared in her cheeks. Even in the dark he could see it. "Apologies," she whispered. "I shouldn't have said that."

But he only smiled. Honestly, he liked it. Which only made him back away. He didn't want to like anything else about Miss Emma Blake. "Don't apologize to me."

"Thank you," she whispered. "For stopping that..." She waved her hand toward where Marsden had disappeared. "And for your kind words."

"You're welcome," he said as he looked back in the ballroom. He ought to find his brother. He shouldn't have left. "Will you be all right?"

She gave a quick nod as she swiped her tears away. "I'm fine. I should return before I'm missed."

"Good idea." But there was a part of him that wouldn't mind staying out here with her all night. Still, he let her go, watching her enter the ballroom and disappear into the crowd.

CHAPTER THREE

EMMA WOKE THE NEXT MORNING, sighing with relief that she'd survived the night and that the entire ordeal of the soirée was over.

The sun was high in the sky, and she could only hope that all the guests had left...two in particular: Lord Marsden and his father.

Even thinking about Marsden made her shiver. Their estate was a half-day's ride north from their property, so they'd stayed the night and would return home today.

If she dallied in her room long enough, they'd surely be gone when she emerged. And she'd make it her goal to never see Marsden again.

But those hopes were quickly dashed. The moment she'd swung her feet over the side of the bed, the door to her room flew open, her mother sweeping in.

The woman sparkled in the late morning light, looking as fresh as if she'd slept the night away rather than staying up all hours.

"Good morning, darling," her mother said with a breezy smile that had Emma's stomach clenching with worry. She'd avoided sharing the details of what happened, because once Marsden was gone, they were irrelevant.

While Emma's body and features resembled her mother's, her

coloring was her father's. Her mother had thick, dark hair that had only just begun to streak with grey. "Good morning."

"I've the best news." Her mother crossed to the vanity and patted the chair for Emma to sit.

Emma stood, slowly crossing the room as she looked her mother up and down, trying to decide what fresh hell was in store for her. "What news?"

"You've managed to secure some further interest." Her mother reached for the ivory-handled brush that sat on the vanity and waved for Emma to come closer.

Her stomach dropped. "Lord Marsden."

"That's right," her mother gushed as Emma slid into the chair, swallowing down a thick lump of dread.

"How long?"

"What do you mean?" her mother asked, untying the ribbon in her hair and removing the plait in which Emma had slept.

"How long will Lord Marsden be staying?" Her hands curled into fists in her lap as she glanced back at her mother.

"A week," her mother answered, her gaze sliding away from Emma's. "Perhaps longer, depending on how the visit unfolds."

And by that her mother meant depending on whether or not he offered for her hand. "I don't want to marry him."

"Nonsense." Her mother pushed her chin straight, beginning to brush her hair again. The bristles, at first gentle, were now raking through Emma's thick strands.

"Honestly, I don't." Desperation was clawing at her throat. "He kissed me last night."

The brush stopped. "Should I demand he wed you?"

"No," she cried, jumping up from the seat. "It was awful. He held me in place so roughly and..." She started to roll the sleeves of her night rail, sure there were bruises on her arms from Marsden's grip.

"Emma," her mother cut in, her hands coming to her hips. "You always do this."

"Do what?" she asked, crossing her arms, her sleeves forgotten.

"Make a big fuss. You'll not say outrageous things or act flamboyantly. For once, you'll behave."

She opened her mouth to protest. She was like a fox in the hunt. Who could blame the animal for running, for fighting?

But her mother held up a finger, stopping her from speaking at all. "And you'll attend tea with our guests today," she said.

"Tea?" she asked, the single word coming out like she'd choke on the liquid rather than drink it.

Her mother let out a huff of air. "Yes. Tea."

"I…" She swallowed down a lump. "I can't."

"You will."

She shook her head, coming up with an excuse as fast as she could. "I promised our new neighbor, Lady Smith, that I'd attend tea with her."

Her mother's gaze narrowed as she gave Emma a long stare, clearly scenting the lie. "Tea with the Smiths?"

"That's right," Emma said, forcing her hands to be still so they didn't give her away. "But I'll see our guests at dinner, I'm certain." Unless she grew ill. The pox would be preferable to dinner with Marsden.

"You'll take Judith."

Emma inwardly groaned. Judith was her mother's watchdog. Technically, she was her personal maid, but Judith had always acted as a second set of eyes for her mother.

It was too late now to back out, though, and so she gave a nod of consent. "Of course."

"I've half a mind to come with you."

Emma's heart jumped in her throat. She'd already invited herself to tea at the Smiths, and while she suspected that Lady Smith would help her keep up the ruse, she hoped to catch Lord Triston in conversation as well. She needed to thank him.

He'd protected her the night before and then he'd held her with such tender comfort…

Lord Triston was so formidable it had been almost shocking how gentle his arms had been. Was she mistaken?

Had it been her imagination or had his very strong arms been the most comfortable spot in which she'd ever found herself?

———

TRIS WIPED the sweat from his brow, hoping that he'd exercised enough to work out the discontent that had kept him up most of the night.

He shouldn't want Emma. She was trouble and he knew it.

No woman of the peerage would ever fit into his world. There was too much darkness in his past for a woman like her to suffer his company and even if that weren't true, he needed a woman who might understand him.

He snorted. What was he saying, he needed no woman at all. At least not one on any permanent basis.

He was a man made *by* and *for* the darkness.

He tossed the towel aside and left the stable to return to the house. He'd like a hot bath and then perhaps the oblivion of a stiff drink or two before he put himself to bed.

Just as he always did for training, he'd untucked his shirt, the neck open to allow his skin to breathe. The summer heat made his skin clammy and damp, and for a moment, he considered shucking the shirt.

He walked slowly, his muscles worn from the activity as the sun shone down on him.

The distant sound of a carriage pricked at his ears. He stopped, shading his eyes as he peered down the lane.

Who would be coming? Was this some sort of threat?

Renewed energy pulsed through him as he started toward the drive once again. Whoever came would face him long before they made it anywhere near the house.

A stately carriage rounded the bend, crossing over the small stone bridge. A meandering stream curved around one side of the property so that every person who came by road had to come just this way. Whichever of Abby's ancestors who'd built the home had made the property pleasing and safe.

But his diligence today was hardly necessary. The carriage was Emma's—or more likely, her father's. But he recognized the vehicle from the last time she'd come to deliver the invitation to that damned soirée.

Was she hosting another party? He'd have to return to London if that were the case. Send his brother Gris here to babysit.

The man's gin business could go to the devil. Tris would take over the gaming hell and start scouting locations for his boxing club.

He crossed his arms as he planted his feet wide.

The carriage drew to a stop, a footman hustling from the seat on the back to open the door. Sure enough, Emma descended the steps, looking so lovely he momentarily forgot his trumped-up irritation.

Her hair had been loosely pulled back, highlighting the thick waves, a few pieces framing her face. Her pale green muslin gown floated about her, skimming all those curves and highlighting her eyes. She gave him a large smile, her face so open and inviting that he found himself standing straighter, his jaw tightening as he prepared himself against the onslaught of warmth starting to creep through him.

"Lord Triston," she called with a wave. "How wonderful to see you."

"What are you doing here?" he asked, knowing full well he was being rude. It was one thing to save her from some thug of a lord, but that didn't make them friends.

She faltered, her hand dropping. "I'm here to have tea with Lady Smith."

He relaxed the slightest bit then. "Tea?"

"Yes. Tea," she answered, clasping her hands, with a pleasant smile.

"So there is no social event you've come to invite us to?" he said, walking closer then, wanting to see her face more clearly. He had to make certain she was telling the truth.

"Goodness no," she laughed. "One a year is all I can manage."

His brows drew together. What did that mean? Didn't ladies plan one event after another? Flitting from one frivolity to the next? "That is the only event you'll host?"

She gave him a quizzical glance and tipped her chin to the side. "Well, we have family for Christmastide and then we'll travel to London for the season." The smile slipped from her face then as she looked down at her feet.

"You don't like London?" Why had he asked that question? He didn't need to know anything else about her.

"I like London just fine. It's the season I don't look forward to."

He raised his brows, because he'd assumed all of society liked the season. "Why not?"

She shrugged, then looked away. "I seem to be too troublesome for a good showing."

He didn't know exactly what a *good showing* meant but he laughed at the word *troublesome*. She'd certainly landed herself in trouble last night.

Then again, he wasn't precisely known for being good. He did knock in men's teeth for sport.

Her gaze skimmed down his frame, stopping at the open V in the neck of his shirt. She visibly swallowed.

He tried not to notice, and even harder tried not to like her reaction. Still, he reasoned that any man liked it when a beautiful woman admired him. Even if that woman was a troublesome minx. Maybe especially when she was a minx.

"Lady Emma," Abby called from the top of the stairs. "I'm so glad you're here."

Emma turned to his sister-in-law, giving her a delightful smile. "I'm glad to have come." And then she was walking toward Abby, her hands extended in greeting as the two women clasped hands.

His brother Rush had married a lady. One with a large dowry and even larger property. He looked back to the lovely home and lands where his brother now lived. It was possible...

But Abby had no family and the circumstances had been unusual. Triston's gaze landed back on Emma. Even if he wished to court her, he'd likely end up at the end of some man's pistol for even trying.

Then again, Rush had had to fight a duel to win his wife.

Rush came out to greet Emma as well and he grudgingly joined the group. His gaze landed on Tris. "Training?"

He gave a quick nod, but Emma looked back at him, her eyes filled with curiosity. "Training for what?"

"He's a pugilist," Abby answered.

"Really?" Emma's eyes widened, her breath visibly catching as she turned more fully toward him.

He straightened. Why did his boxing career incite women's interest? The fact that he regularly hit people shouldn't be so interesting to them. Ladies should be frightened. Instead, they were always flitting about him.

"Are you competing in the fight in Huntington on Saturday?" Emma asked, sounding casual enough. But he watched as she lifted a hand, tracing the neckline of her gown. His jaw hardened. He'd not be drawn in by those sorts of feminine wiles. What was more, she needed to be taught a lesson. Didn't she know that women such as herself got far more than they bargained for with men like him? He'd not treat her as Marsden had, but he could scare her away without laying a single finger on her. Of that, he was certain.

Because she was dangerous. She'd had him actually contemplating marriage for a moment and he knew that if he wasn't careful, didn't frighten her away…

But his gaze followed her gloved fingers, unable to look away.

"He is," Rush answered. "I think he'll do even better here than he normally does in London. The country air is good for the lungs."

Tris snorted. "It's not the air that's good for training, it's the boredom. There is nothing else to do here but exercise."

Emma gave a soft laugh, her eyes sparkling, and he couldn't even deny that the sound was captivating.

He dropped his arms. "Which is why I should get back to it." So much for his hot bath. More training for him. The exhaustion he'd felt minutes ago was gone. Instead, he'd grown hectic inside once again. And after another good round of exercise, he might very well take a cold swim in that river.

It was the only thing that would cool his heating skin.

CHAPTER FOUR

EMMA'S VISIT with Lady Smith had been a delight. The woman was warm, kind, and sweet. They'd discussed nothing of real consequence, but by the time Emma left with her mother's maid in tow, Emma was certain she'd made a friend.

And Abby had not mentioned that their visit had been unplanned, which meant Judith had relaxed and didn't seem bothered when Emma asserted that she'd walk home.

"Walk? Whatever for?" Judith had wrinkled her nose in distaste.

"The foliage is beautiful," Emma had said breezily. She didn't mention that she did not wish to be home, and she intended to stay away from the Northville estate for as long as possible.

Judith had allowed the footman to hand her into the carriage and then had stuck her head back out. "Don't dawdle."

And then the door had snapped shut.

"I'll dawdle if I please," Emma said to no one in particular as she started down the long drive that led from Upton Falls to her own home. "Judith is not my keeper."

She crossed the lovely little stone bridge that passed over the river, but stopped when she reached its apex. Several boulders sat about a hundred feet away, creating a small waterfall just upstream. She'd always loved this spot.

She drew in a lungful of fresh air. What if she just never returned home? What if she just slipped away, traveled to London?

Could she gain a position as a tutor or nanny? Anything had to be better than staying here and allowing Marsden to court her.

She let out a long breath, sticking her bottom lip out so that the strands of hair in the front of her coiffure danced in the air that she blew.

It was likely a bad plan.

Much as she wanted to escape, she knew so little about surviving on her own. Her elbow came to the stone rail, and she rested her chin on her fist.

But how was she going to avoid Marsden's advances? She hadn't been in the man's company five minutes last night when he'd attacked her.

Could she avoid being alone with him?

They were staying in the same house. It would be difficult at best.

Her thoughts were interrupted when a mass of bubbles started rippling on the surface of the water, and suddenly, a man emerged. His back was to her but even from here she knew precisely who he was—Lord Triston.

She gasped as she straightened, the sight of him shirtless and muscles rippling so fascinating, she couldn't tear her gaze away. His overlong hair streamed down his neck, his arms coming up to swipe the dark locks back from his forehead only highlighting the breadth of his shoulders.

She finished crossing the little bridge, but rather than continue down the road, she started walking the bank as Lord Triston dipped back under the water so that only his head appeared above the surface.

"Fine day for a swim," she called as she closed the distance between them.

He turned toward her, that frown etched onto his mouth and forehead as he grimaced at her. "What are you doing here?"

Well, didn't that just make her feel welcome? "It's also a fine day for a walk. One must find ways to keep busy in the country."

He didn't respond as he scrubbed his hands through his hair a few more times. "What do you want, Lady Emma?"

She paused, standing on the bank close to where he rested in the water. It was likely waist height this time of year and crystal clear, so she had an excellent view of his chest and his legs splayed out which were, regrettably, covered by his breeches.

"I want"—she took a deep breath—"to thank you for last night."

Somehow, his grimace only deepened. "Consider the task completed. I have been thanked."

She let out the breath of air. Why did this man not like her? What had she done in their few brief meetings that made him behave so... coldly? "Don't you wish to ask for a boon in return or..."

"A boon?" he asked, his gaze narrowing. "What would you be able to give me?"

"I don't know." She cocked her head, pressing her finger to her lips as she considered. "You likely don't want any invitations to upcoming events."

"No," Lord Triston said the moment she'd finished speaking. "I do not."

"And a picnic is likely—"

"Don't even think it."

Her lips pressed together. "You don't need to be rude." She likely shouldn't have said those words. Debutantes, the kind who found good matches, did not speak like that. Then again, mayhap if she gave Marsden some of that treatment, he'd disappear. But Marsden had said he liked a challenge, whatever that meant.

He let out a growl. "You are the one who is interrupting my swim."

She huffed with irritation, her hands landing on her hips. "My apologies for wishing to thank you, my lord. How very thoughtless of me."

"This isn't the time for such gestures," he fired back.

"And when is the time?" She took a step closer to the water's edge, stomping her foot. "Please tell me the precise moment to tell a man, 'thank you for saving me from the lecherous embrace of another lord, one I am powerless to stop.'"

He rolled his eyes then. "Your stupid rules. What is wrong with you people?"

"You people?" she asked. "What do you mean 'you people,' Lord Triston? I've news for you, *my lord*, you are one of us."

He positively scowled at her, his lip curling in distaste.

She straightened in triumph, knowing that she'd landed a solid punch, as it were. Well, not an actual hit but a good parry. But even as her chin elevated, her right foot slipped on the muddy bank, sliding through the slick muck, her entire body shifting down the bank.

Suddenly, she lost her footing. Her arms flailed wildly and she pitched toward the water.

With sickening slow motion, she was falling in the river.

———

TRIS STOOD as Emma's arms flapped about. He had a moment where he paused, wondering how she managed to look pretty falling.

Perhaps it was the jiggling breasts…

But as she slipped down the bank, her slippers sliding into the water, he recovered himself and started toward her, catching her by the waist. Her hands came to his shoulders, grasping them as she gasped in a breath.

The bank was slippery and for a moment, he wondered how he was going to make it up the steep incline while keeping her from getting wetter, but he just gave up and hauled her against his body as he made his way up onto the grass.

"Oh," she cried, looking up at him as her arms threaded about his neck. It was the second time he'd had her in his arms in as many days, but this time, he was far more aware of the silky softness of her skin as her bare arms brushed his shoulders and the way her breasts crushed against his chest.

Her lips parted in surprise and she stared up at him, her breath coming out in ragged gasps.

Christ, but he'd like to see her breathing like that in his arms for entirely different reasons. She looked like she was in the throes of a zesty lovemaking session.

There was only one thing to do. He still held her in his arms, her feet not touching the ground as he looked down at her.

"I..." she started, her tongue darting out to lick at her lips. "I'm so sorry. I..."

He held her closer still, her stomach pressed tightly to his, their hips... "You are nothing but trouble."

"Oh. Yes. I suppose that's true. My mother says the same." She peered off into the distance then, catching her lip between her teeth.

He let out a frustrated growl. He had to keep this woman from landing in his arms a third time. If she did, he might not be able to resist those lush lips.

And it was imperative that he stay far away from Lady Emma. He'd been involved with a debutante once. Considered himself in love. But that courtship had ended at the end of her father's pistol.

He didn't have a good record with women of noble birth...

Which was why it was best that he frighten her away now.

"You can put me down," she said, still looking toward the country lane. "I'm sorry again—"

"I thought of how you can repay me," he practically growled out, his voice rough. But it was time this woman learned just how dangerous it was to tempt a man of his ilk. And men like Marsden, too, if she valued her safety.

"How?" she asked, her gaze snapping back to his.

"For two good deeds done, I shall take two kisses, I think." And then he set her down on her feet.

She was tall for a woman, but he towered over her, and he'd meant to. He curved forward, bending her back as his mouth hovered over hers.

He kept his features hard and stern, his muscles rippling against her.

He still wore no shirt and as he wrapped an arm tighter about her, he searched her face, waiting to see the flicker of fear his actions brought.

But as her lips parted, her gaze searching his, what reflected from her eyes wasn't fear but curiosity.

Bollocks, this woman didn't seem to have a single thought to her personal safety. Didn't she know that a shirtless man hulking over her while demanding kisses was something to be feared?

"A kiss?" she asked, her eyes widening, and then her fingers splayed out on his shoulders, giving them a light squeeze. The air between them was charged, she seemed to search every inch of his face. "I'm surprised you would ask. I didn't think you liked me very much."

He gave a definite snort. If his kiss didn't frighten her, his words would. "A man doesn't have to like a woman to enjoy her."

That made her eyes go wide as she gasped, pulling back to stare up into his face.

Good. He'd finally sent the right message: *Stay away. I'm dangerous.*

But then she slid her hands down his arms, tracing his biceps. Her skimming touch sent sparking desire pulsing through him. "Is that so?" she asked. "Does it work that way for women as well? Can they enjoy the kiss of a man they don't like?'

"What?" Was she treating this like a kissing lesson instead of being frightened? What did a man have to do to scare her away?

She'd been frightened of Marsden last night. Of that he was certain. But he wasn't the sort of man who could force his attention on a lady. Not even one as troublesome as Emma.

"There are men who are attractive to me, but they are also rude or annoying. Would I like kissing a man like that?"

"You're missing the point," he said, furrowing his brow. "I don't like you, but I'd still like to kiss you."

He felt her stiffen then, her face turning from his. "Well. I'm glad you made that clear…"

And then she was pushing from his arms, her soggy skirts brushing his bare feet. He tried not to act on the regret that tightened his jaw. "I just meant—"

"I think you were perfectly clear on what you meant." Her chin was high, but her eyes held a glossy look that warned him there may be tears yet to come.

His shoulders dropped. "Men like me and women like you shouldn't mix, Emma. That's what I'm trying to say."

She swallowed, giving a stiff nod. "I won't trouble you again." And then she turned and started toward the road.

He had the ridiculous urge to call her back. Take that kiss. But he held his tongue. The last thing he needed was to end up at the business end of her uncle's pistol. Even though he was a lord now, he was a third son with very little money to his name.

He knew how that story ended. He'd lived it on more than one occasion. Best to let Emma go, hurt as she was, knowing it was better for both of them if she stayed away.

CHAPTER FIVE

EMMA FINISHED the walk home in her heavily waterlogged skirts, tears likely shimmering in her eyes. Lord Triston's words ought not to have hurt so much.

She hardly knew the man.

But somehow when he'd helped her last night, she'd gotten a few ideas. Perhaps that frown was the one he gave all the world, not just her.

And if he protected her, mayhap he liked her.

She still didn't wish to wed, not now while she grieved her father's loss, but someday she'd marry a man of her own choosing. Start a family. And when she did...she wished to understand herself. What did she want in a man? Why was she drawn to Lord Triston? Was he another way in which she just craved trouble?

It seemed so. He was rough and surly and there was a raw edge to him that ought to be frightening. He likely scared many with all those muscles and that fierce scowl.

But another voice reasoned that he'd also rushed to her rescue last night. Held her in comfort.

He'd also saved her from falling all the way into the river today. Granted, he'd attempted to intimidate her as well. Not that he'd been successful. She felt safe with him no matter how he acted. It was in such stark contrast to how she reacted to Lord Marsden that it made her pause.

Lord Triston was a mystery, to be certain. If she puzzled him out, however, she might better understand how to proceed with the rest of her life. The idea seemed farfetched, but it also rang true.

For example, should she listen to her mother and marry some stuffy lord who curbed Emma's tendency toward mischief, or ought she follow her own fancies?

The road turned down a bend and the family graveyard on the edge of the property came into view.

Her sister stood near their father's grave, head bent, bonnet covering her face. "Nat?" she called, stopping on the road.

Natalie lifted her head, her cry echoing down the rolling fields. "Emma, what happened?"

Emma's chin dropped. "I slipped at the edge of the river."

"Oh dear," Natalie said and lifted her skirts, rushing toward Emma. "Mother will have a fit. She loved that gown and she's already irritated that you've not made an appearance all day."

Emma looked down at the lovely frock, now sodden and muddy. "There's likely no saving it."

"No." Natalie stopped in front of her, grimacing. "Our only hope is to hide the evidence and get you changed as quickly as possible.

Natalie brushed a stray lock of her own auburn hair aside as she bent lower to inspect the gown. "I'll help you enter the kitchen and distract anyone who might see you."

Emma sighed. Natalie was two years younger, but always helping Emma out of some scrape or another. "Thank you, Nat. I'm sorry."

"Don't apologize to me," Natalie said as she reached for her hand. "It's the least I can do the way mother—" Natalie stopped. She rarely spoke ill of their mother. Natalie knew how to be demure, how to smile and nod, and keep out of scrapes. As a result, their mother rarely gave Natalie a difficult time.

In fact, their mother was fond of pointing out that Emma had entered society late, thanks to her brash nature, but Natalie had long been ready for the venture. It was Emma who held her sister back.

Emma knew that her sister would likely already be wed at eighteen if the family had not been waiting for Emma to make a match first.

She winced with guilt, knowing that her own desire not to wed right away impacted Nat. "I'm sorry," she repeated, because she had far more than a ruined dress to apologize for.

Natalie shook her head. "Stop. You're fine." Then her sister linked her arm through Emma's. "Let's get you back so you'll be ready in time for dinner. Mother will turn purple if you're late for that."

She let out a long breath. Part of her wished to ask for Natalie's aid. Could her sister help her to remain out of Marsden's grasp? But she didn't wish to burden her sister. Natalie already did enough.

So Emma remained quiet as they finished the walk home and then snuck up the back stairs to her room.

Once there, Natalie pulled the soggy dress from Emma and, layer by layer, they replaced the ruined clothing. Finally, they bundled all the soiled garments and shoved the ball in the bottom of the wardrobe.

"Mother claims that Lord Marsden is interested in pursuing a match."

Emma faltered then, averting her eyes as she chewed on her lip. "So she says."

"Emma." There was a warning in Natalie's voice that had Emma snapping her chin up to look at her sister.

"What?"

"Do you like him?" Natalie reached for her hand, squeezing Emma's fingers.

"Not particularly." She'd not lie. Not to Natalie. Her sister did not wish for Emma to wed just to make her own path easier. But she did understand how Emma seemed to stir mischief wherever she went.

"Just be smart about how you reject him."

"I'm not very good at being smart." Her chest constricted. It wasn't precisely true. She'd always been bold before, but of late she seemed to act out more and more often.

34

Natalie sighed. "Don't provoke and don't break the rules."

Emma murmured her agreement, but an hour later, as she stood next to Lord Marsden in the parlor before dinner, she was repeating the words like a chant.

Because her legs itched to run and her mouth…it was filled with words of dissent.

She clenched her teeth together to keep those words in when Marsden reached a hand behind her to rest his palm on the mantel. "You should see Clearview. The land alone would leave you breathless."

"I'm sure it's stunning." Emma had not strung more than four-word answers together since she'd entered the room, which everyone but her seemed to find preferable.

"It is. Twice as large and much more beautiful than the Northville estate."

She didn't roll her eyes. And frankly, she was proud of that fact as she mumbled some nonsensical answer.

Which was the moment his fingers slid from the mantel and onto her base of her neck.

She made to jerk away but his grip was remarkably tight. His voice dropped, low and gravelly, as he leaned close. "We were rudely interrupted last night."

She swallowed down her shiver of revulsion and the words that sprang to her lips. She'd found that interruption most opportune.

Which only made her think of Lord Triston. He'd been clear that he didn't like her. And she shouldn't like him either.

But as Marsden leaned closer still, she realized she'd give anything to have Lord Triston here now. His presence made her feel warm and safe. Didn't anyone else notice the way Marsden was manhandling her?

His breath blew sour across her face. "What say you to a carriage ride tomorrow or the next day?"

She swallowed down a lump of disgust. Even with chaperones, she'd not allow Marsden to take her anywhere. Sliding backwards, he let her go, and she met her sister's concerned gaze across the room.

"Rain is in the air," she said. "I don't think tomorrow would be good, and the next day…"

"What about the next day?" he asked, sounding irritated. She ignored the noise, taking another half step back. She was always in retreat with this man.

"I have plans with Lady Smith."

"Again?" her mother huffed, stepping up next to her. Emma slumped in relief. At least Marsden would keep his hands to himself with her mother by her side.

She gave a quick nod. "Nat too. She's invited us both on an outing."

Nat's brows drew together as she approached the group as well, her uncle and Lord Berwick following behind. Emma didn't mean to burden her sister, but she couldn't have Judith accompany her again.

Lady Smith had not invited her anywhere. And Judith could never see the one place she wished to go—because she planned to attend a boxing match.

"Where are we going?"

"Just a bit of shopping," Emma answered as evasively as possible. She needed some excuse to be gone for the day and she didn't like actual shopping. It was dreadfully boring.

And besides. She'd like to tell Lord Triston that she didn't like him either. And then she'd give him his requested kiss, because he'd earned it, and then she'd be done with the man forever.

She was doing as Nat asked and attempting to avoid trouble.

But a voice told her that her plan was flawed. If she were good, she wouldn't see Lord Triston again, wouldn't kiss him, and most certainly wouldn't watch him box.

But then again, to stay home would mean a carriage ride with Marsden. She'd take her chances at the match…flying fists seemed far safer.

———

Two days after rescuing Emma, Tris arrived in the center of Huntington, noting that a crowd was already forming despite the fact that the match did not start for two more hours.

He always liked to arrive early. It allowed him to get a feel for the space before people crowded it in.

And this event was sure to draw a large crowd. Huntington was home to Maxwell Winter, a renowned fighter despite the fact he was still young.

A year from now, Tris wasn't certain he'd win against the man. But today...he had a good chance.

Either way, the fight would bring in a good paycheck. All money he could use for his own club.

But it would be better if he won.

A man was only as good as his reputation, and as this may very well be one of his last fights, he'd like to finish his career on a strong note.

Some fighters tried to carry on, but when the body began to decline, a man ended up hurt in body, mind, and memory.

He walked around the area that had clearly been marked off in the center square. In a few hours, carriages would line the streets, people crowding the grassy area around the scratched-out spot for the fight.

He drew in a deep gulp of air.

The sun would still be high in the sky, and he'd have to be careful to keep the light at his back.

These were the things an older fighter thought of. One corner was in the shade, and he returned to his vehicle to retrieve his crate before sending the footman off to the stables with his phaeton. He'd sit here between rounds, staying out of the sun that would drain his energy.

In another hour, he'd use the branches of the tree to complete some pull-ups and perform a few other exercises to warm his muscles. He didn't like to start cold.

Rubbing his neck, he crouched down, searching for dips or divots in the ground. The flat ground looked smooth enough and he stood, rolling his shoulders. It was good ground for a fight.

But as he bobbed his head back and forth, loosening his neck, two women caught his gaze across the square as they walked together.

Both had thick auburn hair artfully arranged at the back of their bonnets. They stopped, and the taller of the two turned, meeting his eye. She was far enough away that he couldn't see the details, but he could feel her gaze and he knew precisely who looked at him.

Emma.

The awareness of knowing slid down his spine, tightening his muscles. How was it that in the dark, or from far away, or underwater, he always knew it was her?

Stalking out of the shade, he started across the square toward her. He wasn't certain why. He had no right to tell her to leave, but she was...a distraction. One he didn't need.

He'd been feeling guilty since the day before yesterday by the river. He hadn't meant to hurt her feelings when he'd blurted out that he didn't like her. All right, he'd meant to hurt them. But he hadn't liked the feeling in his gut when the deed had been done.

He'd reasoned over and over that the act had been necessary. The woman was bound to rain chaos down on his life just when he was finally on a good path. The right path.

He should stay away from Miss Emma Blake. Period—except he kept walking toward her.

"Miss Blake," he gritted out between his teeth as he stalked closer. "What are you doing here?"

She brought her hands to her hips, while the other woman visibly started and slid behind Emma. "Where I go is none of your concern, Lord Triston."

He stopped just a few feet away. "Was I not clear that the two of us should not mix?"

"You are the one that came stomping over to me, my lord."

He blinked, surprise momentarily silencing him. She was completely right. "Only because—"

"And you've frightened my sister. Don't be such a beast."

His jaw clamped shut. The other woman peeked out from behind Emma's shoulder, her wide green eyes filled with fear.

"My apologies." It was one thing to spar with Emma, who, even when he'd tried to make her, hadn't been afraid of him.

"She is far more delicate than me and cannot tolerate your abuse."

"I'm not that—" the other woman started, but Emma held up her hand.

"What's more, since you're here, I may as well say that I've thought about your boon."

His brow furrowed. What was the blasted woman talking about? Was she making sense and he was just distracted by her heaving bosom? It was marvelous. "My boon?"

"That's right. And I've decided I'll not give it. I intended to…but I've decided you're right. It would be best if we never saw one another again."

"Good," he replied, but he didn't exactly like the word on his tongue. It tasted bitter.

"Fine," she said back, her chin notching even higher. "Perfect."

Crossing his arms, he scowled. "I don't need the bother you bring anyway."

She dropped her chin then, pressing her hands to her stomach.

He knew he'd hurt her feelings again, but he ignored that bit of nagging guilt. It really was better for both of them if they went their separate ways. He had goals and she had some bright and shiny future that didn't include a man who'd been raised on the docks.

"You're not a bother, Emma," the other woman whispered, but he heard it anyway. "Don't listen."

But Emma shook her head. "We both know that I am, Nat." Then she looked back at him with sad eyes, the kind that cut him to the bone. The fact that she fully believed the words meant to wound made an ache pulse in his chest. "Good day, Lord Triston. Best of luck with your fight."

And then she turned back to her sister and linked her arm through the other woman's before walking away.

He watched her retreat, standing in the sun, wondering once again if he'd done the right thing. He knew how affairs with such women ended. He'd attempted to have them more than once.

But somehow, he still hated to see her go.

CHAPTER SIX

EMMA WAS NOT STAYING in the village to see the fight. Most definitely not. She was done with Lord Triston. Absolutely.

But she found her gaze routinely moving to the square, watching the swell of the crowd.

And anyway, she couldn't see either fighter. Too many people stood between her and the scratched-out square.

Nor could she hear anything beyond the jeers and calls of the many men packed into the town center, but she knew he was there. And somehow, knowing that he'd also be hurt, hit and kicked, she couldn't bring herself to leave Huntington.

"Emma." Nat pulled her sleeve. "Don't you think we should return home? It's getting late."

"Likely, yes," she answered, not looking at her sister. In the willow that flanked the ring, several boys swung from the branches to get a better view. They looked so carefree, and she had a moment of jealousy. Were that she was a boy and able to just climb trees and frolic instead of being expected to follow the rules and sit still all the time.

"Then why don't we—"

"Because." She looked at Natalie, willing her sister to understand.

"There is something about him." She still couldn't shake the feeling that he was some key meant to unlock her future.

Natalie frowned. "Emma."

"I know," she sighed. "He's no good and I am likely repeating my usual pattern of putting myself in the exact position in which I ought not to be."

Natalie nipped at her lip. "Maybe."

Emma closed her eyes, wanting someone to understand the position in which she found herself. And if anyone would, it was Natalie. "Lord Marsden trapped me on the balcony at the soirée," she whispered, not wishing for anyone else to hear. "And then he kissed me."

"What?" her sister cried, tugging harder on her sleeve.

"It was dreadful and cruel and..." Her gaze dropped to the ground. "And Lord Triston came to my aid."

"Oh," Natalie gasped as her fingers circled Emma's upper arm. "I had no idea."

She shook her head. "I can't leave here because I am worried that he'll be hurt."

"Em, this is his occupation. He's fought many times before."

"I know," she said, scanning the crowd once again. "But all the same..." She shook her head. They were bound together in some way and despite knowing she should break that bond, she just couldn't seem to do it. "And besides, what waits for me at home? Marsden? Mother?"

Natalie's fingers loosened, beginning to rub circles on her arm. "We can stay a bit longer, I suppose, but not too much. Remember... we're going to thread the needle, so to speak, with this entire situation. You're going to avoid Marsden without catching mother's ire."

Emma huffed. "There's little chance of that."

"Still." Natalie started to pull her toward the crowd. "Let's do our best, shall we?"

"You're right," she said as she let Natalie pull her closer. They'd remain on the outskirts of the action, but perhaps if they were closer, she could at least hear what was happening. Be reassured that Triston was all right.

But as they moved under the willow, she noted that the boys she'd seen earlier could see everything from their vantage point.

"Look at how large Lord Triston is," one of them called to another.

"Massive," another replied.

"Not as big as our Max," another said, sounding irate.

"Bigger," yet another called. "And so calm. How can he be so calm?" The excitement was palpable among the boys in the tree.

Emma cocked her head as she studied the tree. It didn't look so hard to climb. And if she made it to even the first branch, she'd be able to see Triston. The overwhelming urge to join them made her chest tight. Would it be as freeing as it seemed?

With her eye on Triston, might she relax a bit? She'd certainly know if he was seriously injured if she could watch him.

"Hello," she called up into the trees. "How did you get up there?"

The boys quieted, likely certain they were in trouble.

"Emma," Natalie hissed, tugging on her arm once again. She shook her sister off, studying the tree, noting the knot a few feet up on the trunk.

"If I start to climb, will one of you pull me up?" she asked as she tried to gauge the distance. The much shorter boys had made the climb.

"Yes, ma'am," one called.

"Don't do it," Natalie cried. "This is exactly how you manage to take yourself from the frying pan into the fire."

But she didn't pay her sister any mind. Emma had decided, and besides, the crowd was too loud for anyone to hear her. Everyone was looking at the fighters. Surely no one would notice...

Stretching up, she reached for the thick branch, planting her booted foot on the knot. Two of the boys grabbed her elbows, and grunting, they hauled her up so that her stomach pressed into the branch as she balanced on the limb with her body.

Her stomach ached and she let out a grunting breath, but she could see everything.

Lord Triston stood in one corner, his back to her as he readied to begin. Diagonally across from him stood another barrel-chested man who danced back and forth while punching the air.

Seeing him so calm and ready made her limp with relief and she wilted over the branch.

But Emma stiffened once again as a bell rang out, sending the crowd into a frenzy. The fight was about to begin.

————

TRISTON SPIT as he sized up the other man. Strong enough, Max Winter might make a good opponent someday. If Triston were to guess, he'd mostly fought men who were smaller, because he didn't understand the first thing about conserving energy.

Dancing and yelling to the crowd, he'd be tired before he even threw a punch. Which meant Triston knew exactly how to fight him.

The bell clanged and Tris started for the center of the ring. He let Winter dance, shout, and even allowed him a few swings that Tris ducked before he popped a quick tight fist right into the man's face.

The jolt of the hit shot down his arm when his knuckles crunched into Winter's nose, blood instantly spurting from both nostrils like a water spigot.

Winter stumbled back, his eyes wide, before he recovered himself and charged at Triston like an angry bull.

Tris might have *tsk*ed. Anger burned too much energy and it made a man foolish. Winter had much to learn yet, which meant that Triston easily sidestepped the charge, shoving the other man as he passed.

But Winter recovered more quickly than Tris had anticipated and spun around, landing several quick blows to his midsection.

The hits sounded in his ears, soft flesh against hard as his body doubled over in pain. Every fighter knew how to keep his stomach clenched to absorb the shock, but it still hurt like hell as the power of the punches rocked through him.

He blew out hard and fast to recover from the pain, taking a sharp jab at the man's chin, and was rewarded when his fist made contact, Winter's head snapping back as his teeth audibly clanked together.

On and on they fought, Triston wearing the other man down slowly and methodically. He could see the tiredness pulling at Winter's eyes even as the man attempted to keep his chin up. Winter had spirit. Tris could give him that.

But a few body shots and Triston could feel the other man's core muscles weakening under his fists.

He took a step back like he'd retreat but then rushed forward again, pulling his right arm back and letting it fly into Winter's face.

Pain exploded in his own hand while Winter's hand flew out, grasping at air, and then the other fighter fell flat on the ground.

Triston stood over him, waiting to see if he would rise as the crowd roared its approval.

He shook his head.

Years ago, he'd fed off the crowd too. But people were fickle, cheering for Triston even when their local fighter lay knocked out on the ground.

Which was why all his fight energy now came from within.

He looked up, lifting his arms, taking his victory a moment before he made his way to his corner, sitting on a crate as ten men or more slapped his shoulders and back in congratulations.

He gave a cursory nod of thanks. Fighting had always channeled his raw aggression, the anger that had itched at his skin.

And he still liked the physical training, but he was right to want to retire. Tris could feel it in this moment of victory, which should have been filled with raw excitement. Instead, he felt only the most cursory satisfaction. He didn't love the fight the way he used to. Winning today had been necessary for his next venture, he knew that. The joy, however, was gone.

Slowly the crowd thinned, many going on to celebrate in the tavern.

Winter was hauled up, bruised, taken home to recover. Triston would speak with him in a day or two. He could help Winter be a better fighter and perhaps the man could become his first client.

When much of the crowd had dissipated, he rose from his crate, stretching aching muscles as he picked up the wooden box, intent to find the footman and his phaeton.

It was time to make his way home.

A ring of ladies stood on the other side of the square, umbrellas twirling as they eyed him with interest. Fans snapped, and one brunette was bold enough to wink.

He gritted his teeth and turned away. He had no interest in the fluttering flock of admirers. They were all the same. Eyelashes that artfully batted at him. Soft voices, coy touches, and easy bedmates. But after…

"Lord Triston," a female called from far closer than the group of women across the square.

His gnashed his teeth and didn't bother to look up at whatever bold lady approached. "Go away."

"I would, my lord, but Emma is stuck and…"

His gaze snapped up to find Emma's sister in front of him. She jumped back when their eyes met, and he attempted to soften his expression. He knew he frightened her. "Stuck where?"

She pointed her finger up and that's when saw her…or at least her boots and skirts dangling down from the very branch he'd use to do pull-ups. Her feet kicked back and forth, swishing her white petti-coats like fabric blowing in the breeze.

Taking a step back, he saw the rest of Emma on the other side of the branch, her behind stuck up in the air as she grasped the branch with both arms. "A few whelps helped me up, but they all scattered before any of them had the decency to get me down."

"Woman," he gritted out, his jaw locked. Whether his irritation stemmed from her ability to get herself in the most ridiculous situa-tions or that fact that her derriere looked delightful in that position he did not examine. "You are—"

"Don't say it. I know. I'm a mess. Would you berate me after you help me down, please? My stomach hurts something fierce."

He let out a long-suffering rush of air as he reached up for her legs.

But before he could grab them, Natalie let out a scream. His attention snapped to her a moment before a fist landed hard in his side.

He doubled over, wondering that the hell had just happened.

CHAPTER SEVEN

EMMA bit back the scream that filled her lungs as two men jumped onto Triston's back.

She didn't know who either of them was, nor did she care. He was already exhausted, and she watched in horror as he fell to the ground, the other two men pummeling his face and body with their fists.

Natalie cried out and darted behind the tree, but Emma dragged in a gulp of air and wiggled her torso so that her feet hung down lower, her body barely staying on the branch. Her arms clenched with the effort of holding her position. Still, she waited until one of the men had moved to the spot just below her boots and then she let go.

She hit his back, not with her boots but with her torso, the force greater than she'd imagined. The air punched from her lungs, her body exploding in pain even as she tried to hold on to the man's back.

She failed and fell to the side, her ankle twisting under her own weight. A keening wail of pain erupted from her lips as she tried to grab at the injured leg, but the man fell too, landing half on top of her as she cried out again, her leg twisting further.

Triston let out a guttural roar that echoed about the square. The sound frightened her as he tossed the other man, the one he'd been grappling with, to the side.

Surprise stopped her own cries as she watched the man fly through the air. And then Triston grabbed the other man still on top of her by the scruff of his collar, dragging him several feet away.

The first assailant rushed at Triston again, but not letting go of the other, his fist shot out, punching the first man hard in the face.

She lifted a hand to cover her mouth. Even tired and beaten, Triston easily subdued the two men. Her heart raced wildly in her chest as she watched him, face hard, muscles bulging, as he pulled the man he held up by the collar, his face only an inch away as he gritted out through clenched teeth, "Tell me your game."

"No game," the man managed to push out as his head snapped back and forth. "Guiltmore had an offer—"

"Guiltmore," he spat. "The solicitor who has been plaguing my family?"

"Not plag-plaguing, my lord. He's only trying to buy your club."

"By threatening and attempting to kidnap women?" Triston shook him hard again, the man's head rattling back and forth.

"I don't know anything about that."

"Then why are you here?" Triston cuffed the man across the cheek as though he'd accept nothing but the truth. Part of her knew she ought to be scared. Triston's power was undeniable, but there was something so safe in his size. His strength.

A woman might just be secure enough next to a man like that to really explore who she was and what she wished to be.

"To deliver a message." The criminal raised his hands in a silent plea.

"Spit it out."

"All-all-all right." The other man held Triston's wrists even as Tris continued to shake him. "Meet him this Friday at the East India Docks, Blackwall Yard. Midnight."

A meeting? With other nefarious men? Her heart climbed into her throat as she looked at Triston. He wouldn't go, would he?

She hated the idea of him being in danger, and selfishly, she didn't want him in London. She wished for him to be here.

———

TRIS GRUNTED, letting the man go before raising his fist and crashing it into the criminal's face.

He didn't even bother to see how it landed before he turned, striding toward Emma, who still lay in a heap. Fear thundered through him to see her crumpled on the ground like that, her face twisted in pain.

"Infernal woman," he snapped as moved toward her, knowing he sounded more angry than frightened. But she ought not to put herself in danger like that. "What were you thinking?"

She grimaced as she clutched at her ankle. "You were in trouble."

"I am perfectly capable of taking on a few common thugs. You are not." But his chest tightened all the more at her words. They touched something inside him. Emma was a different sort of woman. He'd lumped her in with the rest of the peerage the first few times he'd been with her. But the longer he knew her, the more he could see she wasn't like those ladies who batted their eyelashes and then ran at the first sign of trouble.

She saw things through, was resilient, and recognizing and admiring those qualities would get *him* in trouble.

"But they were on top of you." She tilted her chin up to him, her hair tumbling from her pins and over her shoulders as her green eyes clouded with worry. The column of her neck was exposed—the fichu covered her cleavage, but he could imagine it.

He let out a loud breath of frustration, at her and at himself. "I was about to throw them both."

"Oh," she whispered in a voice that trembled. "I thought I was helping."

He dropped to one knee, flipping up her skirts.

Not only did her ankles look fine, they were delightfully slender, her calves rounded in the prettiest way. His fist tightened as he resisted the urge to slide his hand over the flesh, check for injuries, learn the shape of her.

His gaze lifted to hers as she winced. Pain? Regret?

He gently grasped the foot, her short boot keeping him from seeing the lower flesh that met her foot. "How bad does it hurt?" Even he could hear how his voice had softened.

"It'll be fine. I only twisted it. Not my first time." Then she looked away. "I'm sure you're not surprised by that fact."

He wasn't. She ran headlong into danger with surprising courage. He moved the foot, slowly and carefully testing the joint, but she didn't wince. Her silky stockings slid under his hand and he blew out the frustrated air holding in his lungs. Because he was irritated—she'd put herself in danger but she had also impressed him, and he would not be one more person who made her feel worse about herself.

Even he, who was not the most observant person, could see that Emma was regularly informed of how badly she behaved, and it ate at her. "You were very brave," he added quietly.

"Oh," she said, her breath catching.

Then he looked up into her bright green eyes again. How many women would have done such a thing? Hell, how many men?

He hadn't needed her help, so why did it seem to matter so much that she'd given it?

Reaching under her, he pulled her against his chest, lifting her into his arms. Her hands wrapped about his neck as all that softness nestled into the hard planes of his body.

The answer to his own question hit him with more force than a good uppercut to the chin.

She was better than the rest of them. The peerage he didn't like. The criminals who'd cut a man just as soon as they'd help him. She rose up above, special and unique. Honest, brave, and so damned beautiful.

She was so much more than the countless women who'd come and gone from his life. When had any of them ever tried to save him?

Those ladies had wanted his strength, his success. But none of them had ever wanted the darker parts like his heritage or his temper. But Emma...she wasn't afraid of him in the least and she didn't run when some ugly part of his life showed itself.

Her head rested against his shoulder.

"Natalie," he called, assuming that was the woman's full name. Emma's sister stepped out from behind the tree, her chin tucked down, hands twisted together.

"Is everyone all right?" Natalie asked, kicking at the dirt with her boot.

"Fine," he answered, looking down at Emma. Her eyes had fluttered closed but that didn't stop him from admiring the dark fringe of her lashes on her cheeks, the pretty slope of her jaw, the delicate lobe of her ear.

And her eyes opened, and she smiled back at him, her grin so sweet and sexy that it stole the air from his lungs.

"Emma?" Natalie asked.

"Just a twisted ankle. Mother is going to be furious."

"At least we'll have a plausible reason for arriving home late," Natalie reasoned.

Tris studied the other girl; she had much of Emma's same beauty but with far less fire. All at once, he knew that Emma's spunk was one of his favorite things about her. He liked it even more than the ample breasts currently crushed against his chest.

"Let's go," Emma sighed. "With any luck, the doctor will force me to stay abed for the rest of the week."

"Why would that be lucky?" he asked, scanning for their carriage.

"So she can avoid Lord Marsden, of course."

His gaze snapped back to Emma, anger that should have long burned out of him coursing through him. That man was still at her home? How had he not known about this? "Marsden?"

Emma shot her sister a withering look.

"Marsden isn't gone?"

"No." Natalie shook her head. "Though Em is right. If her ankle is bad enough, she'll be abed, and then Marsden and Berwick will likely leave."

He eased his grip on her a bit, some of her actions the past few days cast in a new light. Had she been avoiding Marden and that was why she kept appearing? Had she not been specifically seeking him out?

He pushed his disappointment away. He might like her better now, see how different she was, but that didn't mean he was going to toss away his future for a debutante with a penchant for disaster.

He had a solid plan to start a club and that meant he could not support a wife even if he wished for one. Which he didn't.

But as he looked down at her, his chest tightened all over again and a nagging thought tickled the back of his mind.

She belonged in his arms.

CHAPTER EIGHT

"Lord Triston?" Emma asked as they moved toward her family carriage. Natalie climbed inside as Triston slowed his steps.

"Tris," he replied.

She blinked in surprise. They were having another of those soft moments. The ones that seemed to come when she needed them most. "Tris?"

"That's right."

When he spoke like that, all warm and deep, her insides melted. Which made the next words even harder to say. "I won't bother you again. I promise."

She looked at his shoulder, the one flexing under her weight. She'd like to run her hand over it, feel the ripple of his muscles.

He let out a long breath that made her wince. Which is why his words caught by her surprise. "You can bother me, Emma. In fact, if anything happens and you need help, you come straight to me, you hear?"

Her gaze flew to his again, her lips parting in surprise. She searched his face for answers but instead of finding them, she grew even more confused as he bent so close, their mouths almost touching.

"I mean it. Tell me you'll come for me if you need me."

"I will," she answered, completely overwhelmed. His scent was wrapped about her, leather, and sandalwood, and male musk. Her fingers threaded into his hair, his mouth dropped a bit closer.

What was he doing? But his next comment answered her question. "I'm not sure, after your rescue today, that you still owe me a boon, but I'm taking it."

Rescue? He'd said he didn't need help. But she didn't have a chance to ask a single question because his lips descended to hers. Her mouth had been parted to speak but as his lips came over hers, he softly kissed them closed.

The pain in her ankle was completely forgotten as tingling pleasure spread through her. it started at her mouth, but somehow, it carried all the way down to her toes. His lips were warm, and firm, and so masculine that a different kind of ache pulsed between her legs.

He lifted away for just a second and her eyes fluttered open to look up at him. She wished to remember this moment forever…the straight line of his nose, the glittering darkness of his eyes. The strong jaw and hard planes of his face that made him look as though he were strong enough to hold up the whole world.

Could he support hers, the one that felt as though it were crumbling around her?

And then, his mouth so gentle she ached, he kissed her again.

She sighed, wishing this moment might last forever, but all too soon, he lifted his head, turned around, and closed the distance between them and the carriage.

"Your boon is paid, Emma," he said, low and quiet, but the words echoed through her. "And now I owe you one of my own."

"But you didn't need me to save you today," she said and then instantly regretted the words. She'd take the boon. She could collect another kiss or—

"You find me if anything goes amiss. I'm now honor bound to come to your aid."

And then he loaded her into the carriage, sliding her in the seat next to her sister. Without another word, he stepped out again and closed the door behind him.

Long after the carriage began the short drive home, she stared out the window, hoping for one last glance of him.

"Did you see the way he fought both those men?" Natalie asked, craning her neck as well.

Emma turned to her sister, noting a slight flush in Natalie's cheeks. Emma hardly blamed her. Triston did that to a woman. Tris, his brother had called him. She liked the name and after that kiss, she liked the intimacy of knowing this shortened version. "I did."

"The way he carried you."

"I didn't exactly see that part," she answered with a smile. "But I felt it."

Natalie shook her head, looking at Emma with a breathless sort of wonder brightening her eyes. "He's a lord."

"You think he's frightening."

"I think he's very masculine," Natalie replied. "I'm frightened a bit, or I was, but you're not in the least and—"

Emma snorted. "True." But she looked back out the window. "But Nat. He hardly even likes me."

Natalie's mouth twitched. "You don't think so?"

After that kiss, who could say? "And besides. Mother would never approve."

"That is the truth." Natalie scrubbed one of her cheeks. "Still. Maybe once Marsden's gone, she'll come around. His brother is a marquess. Is there family money?"

Emma didn't answer, partially because she didn't know. It had never occurred to her to ask about his finances nor his views on marriage, because she hadn't been considering the institution herself. At least not in the near future.

Would she want to marry Triston? She'd asserted that she didn't wish to wed either. She'd wanted to find her future on her own terms. Without constant judgment, and without a man of her mother's choosing. One whom she'd likely disappoint and might be tempted to keep her in a tight cage as her mother had always done.

But would she want marriage with a man who liked her just the way she was?

Perhaps what she craved most of all was a love that judged her far less and found her worthy.

———

Tris sat in the cold water of the river allowing the water to soothe away the hurt of the aching muscles.

The sun was setting, and he'd been freezing when he'd emerged from the frigid water, but his body required the cold to reduce the swelling.

"Tell me again what's happened," his brother Rush demanded, crouching on the bank above him. Rush was understandably concerned about the attack on Tris. Guiltmore had attempted to kidnap Rush's wife just a month before.

He repeated the story of the attack, sharing everything except the part where he'd kissed Emma.

He still wasn't certain if he'd made the right choice and the last thing he needed was his brother demanding he marry the lady. Though if he were being honest, the idea wasn't as dreadful as it had been a few days before. But he shook his head. His boxing club would never make the money to support Emma in the life to which she was accustomed.

And he'd not take her dowry only to spend the money on supporting her, if her family would even approve the match. It was a man's job to support his wife, not the other way around. He never understood the lords who married a woman for money. Did they have no decency? His father had done that very thing—married a woman, spent her money, all the while filling Rush and Tris's mother with baby after baby while giving almost nothing to support them.

Rush frowned. "Miss Blake launched herself from a tree to come to your aid?"

He gave a stiff nod, the movement splashing water in his face. "That's right."

56

"Hells bells," Rush murmured. "That's quite a woman."

He didn't outwardly agree. But inwardly…he'd come to the same conclusion. "The part we should be discussing is the invitation to a meeting with the solicitor."

"I don't like any of it."

"Me either. But what choice do I have? This is a situation which needs resolving." He ran his hands through his hair as he stretched his legs out under the water.

"I don't think you should go," Rush said, standing.

"Why not?"

"Because." He crossed his arms over his chest. "Why did they come all the way out here to invite you to a meeting in London? Gris and Fulton are in the city. Why not invite one of them?"

It was an excellent question. He'd been so focused on resolving the problem, moving on with his life, that he wasn't properly strategizing. "What are you thinking?"

"They know I won't leave my wife, so you'd be traveling alone. An ambush?"

Triston gritted his teeth as he considered his brother's words. He had to confess that it was smart thinking on Rush's part. "And if I can make it to London without being attacked? Is it possible to end this so we can all return to the city?"

Rush frowned. "I don't like the idea of you going to that meeting alone."

He sat up, water pouring down his shoulders. "I can take Gris and Fulton."

"What about our half-brother, East? He's an earl. Who is going to kill him for a gaming hell?"

Tris grimaced. He didn't like relying on their half-brother. He hated the system that made him dependent on the title for his personal safety and besides, he wasn't a man who needed anyone. Usually. The memory of Emma falling from the tree, trying to help him, flashed through his mind again.

The minx. A smile touched his lips.

"Are you smiling?"

He immediately wiped the grin from his lips, giving Rush a frown. "No."

"Yes, you were." Rush looked him up and down. "Don't do that. You look odd." And then his brother made a face as though he'd smelled something foul.

"You're odd," he replied, too tired and...happy to be really offended. Which should concern him. They were discussing traps, and death, and clubs that brought nothing but trouble. He was trying to finish this business with Guiltmore so that he might start his own life, and all he could think about was Emma.

Rush stared at him, his brows furrowing. "You calling me odd is odd. You grumble, and growl, and hit things..." Rush tapered off, studying Tris in a way that made him uncomfortable. He stood, making his way out of the water.

"I'm too tired for growling," he lied. He was tired. But also, some of the fight had leaked out of him recently and he rather liked the feeling.

"And the meeting?"

"It's a few days away, I'll think on it some more and make a decision tomorrow."

Rush offered Tris his hand to help him up the bank, which he gratefully took. "I'm going to write to East, Gris, and Fulton. See if they have any insight."

Wrapping a blanket about his shoulders, he nodded. "Good idea."

They began walking back toward the house, the darkening sky adding a hush to the landscape. He stopped, looking out over the fields. "I see why you like it here."

Rush lifted a brow. "You're losing your faculties."

"I'm not." He started walking again. But he knew Rush was right. He was going soft. For a woman. With a shake of his head, he pulled the blanket tighter. "I can't check on Emma tomorrow. It wouldn't be acceptable."

"Emma?"

"Miss Blake."

"Right."

"So could you ask Abby? Please?"

Rush's hand came to his shoulder. "Of course."

Soft. That was the word, for certain. But he'd have to toughen himself back up because as soon as this business with Guiltmore was over, he was leaving and returning to London to start a boxing club of his own.

No Emma. No ladies of the peerage and no marriage. Ever. But the words didn't fill his chest with resolve and he trudged back to the house, wondering what path he'd wandered down in his life, because it didn't feel like the one he'd been on before.

"I've changed my mind," he declared, stopping again.

"About what?" Rush asked. "The meeting?"

"No, swimming. My legs need to soak for longer." Truthfully, it was his rushing blood that needed cooling. Emma had that effect on him.

"Suit yourself," Rush grunted. "I'm going back to check on my wife. I don't like leaving her alone."

Tris cocked a brow as he turned back to the water.

What Rush said might be true, but these days, Rush was never very far from his wife's side. Could Tris ever be as committed as his brother?

CHAPTER NINE

EMMA SAT IN HER BED, frowning at the doctor, who talked softly with her mother as though Emma wasn't there at all.

"She'll be fit as a fiddle tomorrow," he assured her mother with a soft pat on her shoulder.

"Thank goodness," her mother replied, a hand to her heart. "I was so worried."

Worried? Was that why her mother had berated her for the entire hour before the doctor had arrived?

Emma had received a stern lecture about how selfish she'd been to go and get hurt when they had this excellent opportunity to win the hand of an earl. It had gone on and on, with a large emphasis on duty and responsibility.

She'd not argued the point. There was nothing to be gained. Her mother wouldn't listen, and she'd only increase the length of the lecture if she were to argue.

Still, she'd hoped that the doctor might share different news. If her foot was well, then Marsden would not leave, he'd remain. And sooner or later, her mother would insist that Emma spend real time with the man. She couldn't avoid him forever—could she?

She remembered Tris's insistence that she find him if she were in trouble. But what if her next incident with Marsden was like the kiss on the balcony? Her heart beat loudly in her chest as her hands fisted in the covers. What if it got worse?

The doctor left, Mother showing him out as Emma watched the last rays of sun disappear from the sky.

She needed a plan. A real one. No more vague notions of not marrying. No more short-gain evasive tactics.

She tapped her chin, attempting to decide what might keep Marsden from pursuing her. Sighing, she sank back into the pillows. She could declare herself ruined. Natalie would make a far better debutante than herself.

But would anyone even believe her? Her mother hadn't listened when she'd tried to explain how vile Marsden had been at the soirée.

What if…she actually was ruined? A vision of Triston rose up in her thoughts.

The very idea of kissing him again, of allowing him to touch her, filled Emma with such excitement that she sat up, tossing the covers off her bed.

After grabbing her dressing gown, she slipped down the back stairs to the kitchen and put on an oversized pair of wellingtons that had been her father's. Then she opened the kitchen door and made her way out into the night.

She knew every inch of the property and she moved easily in the dark, making her way down the lane, past the graveyard lit by moonlight, to the little bridge on the border of Upton Falls.

The water gurgled and tumbled over rocks and, once again, she leaned on the stone walls, looking down into the water.

But she nearly jumped back when she saw a man in the water.

"Tris?" she called, and he immediately turned, his bare chest glistening in the moonlight.

"Emma?"

"It's me." Excitement pulsed through her as she rushed off the bridge and along the bank. "Is the water freezing?"

"No doubt," he said as he moved toward her. "What are you doing here?"

She drew in a shaky breath. "My ankle is fine."

"Good."

Sliding the boots off, she shed the house coat as well and gathered the hem of her night rail in her hands. This time, she sat on the edge of the bank and sank her feet and ankles into the water, gasping in a breath as the cold water rushed over her skin. "How are you able to remain in this ice-cold water?"

He chuckled, though it sounded a bit strained. "It's good for sore muscles. Good for your ankle too."

That seemed as good a reason as any to be here. She'd come because she wished to think through her plan, weigh out the benefits and drawbacks for a change. But it seemed the plan was working itself out.

Her gaze met Triston's as she pulled the hem of her night rail a bit higher. His eyes shifted, taking in the length of her legs, and satisfaction pooled in her stomach.

"But that's not why you're here, is it?"

Drat. So much for excuses. "I don't know why I'm here. I had this crazy idea and…"

"You? I don't believe it."

Heat filled her cheeks. "I know. Everyone says it's true. I'm reckless and impulsive." And then she sank back on her elbows, her chin tilting up to the sky.

"For the record, I like you just the way you are."

Her chin snapped down again, her gaze meeting his. "Even though I got stuck in a tree and jumped on a man's back and—"

"Emma." The gravel of his voice made her shiver as he moved through the water closer to where she rested on the bank. "You're impulsive, yes, but sweet, and generous, and—"

"I want you to ruin me." The words tumbled from her lips before she could stop them.

He stilled in the water. "I beg your pardon."

"I want you to ruin me," she said again, trying to sound sure.

He drew up straighter. "I see." His voice held an edge that was so hard it could have cut glass.

She shook her head. "I know it means I'll never marry. And I'm a bit worried about how it will effect Nat—"

"Did it occur to you that you'd have to marry me?" And then he was moving toward her again. "Or, if not marriage, I could end up in a duel with your uncle?"

She sat straight up with a gasp. "Oh, Triston!"

He stopped just a few feet in front of her. "Tell me now, which one frightens you more?"

Her brow furrowed. Of course she'd be worried about his safety. She'd been in a panic at the fight today. How could he even ask that question?

ANGER PULSED THROUGH TRIS. He'd thought Emma was different. But here she was, wanting him for one thing—a bit of meaningless sex to move her life in the direction of her choosing.

He was only ever a cheap piece of trash. Nothing worth fighting for. Nothing worth holding on to. No one worth marrying.

"I would never allow something bad to happen to you," Emma said the words so quietly he nearly missed them.

And then she was pulling her night rail higher. Past her knees and up to her thighs, the length of her legs exposed.

She clearly walked a great deal, and they were the perfect balance of shapely and muscular. He could spend hours kissing every inch of them…and then higher to the apex of her body.

Even in the cold water, his cock turned stiff as stone and strained against his breeches.

She slipped into the water, then glided over to stand just in front of him. "Why are you so upset?"

He grunted. "You wish to use me."

She blinked in surprise. "But I thought men preferred a quick and meaningless tête-à-tête."

His jaw worked as his teeth ground together. That was an excellent point. And he'd not share his history, of the socially powerful women who'd wanted one thing from him and nothing more. "I am a man who has little money and few prospects, Emma. I can't afford to be impulsive when it comes to meaningless tête-à-têtes."

"Oh. Of course." She lifted a hand toward him and he thought she might touch him, but then she dropped it again. "I'm sorry to have insulted you."

And that was what was lovely about Emma. So kind, so open.

"I just...I'm not sure I want to marry anyone, certainly not a man my mother has chosen, and I don't think she'll stop trying until I force some sort of end—"

"Not marry?" He stared down at her, trying to understand. "Why wouldn't you marry?"

"I don't need a man to replace my mother."

She pulled the hem up a bit higher to keep the cloth from getting wet, her pale thighs visible in the moonlight.

He could just picture those legs wrapped about him. They'd be so smooth and silky.

His cock gave a painful throb.

He took a step closer until only a few inches separated them. Her hair was loosely plaited and hanging over one shoulder, the curled end wrapping around her breast.

He reached out, holding the thick braid in his hand as he let the strands slide over the palm of his hand. It would be so easy to do as she requested. Lay her down on the bank, start kissing every part of her body until she was hot and wanton under his lips.

"Emma, do you have the funds to remain unwed?"

Her eyes widened. "I think so. I don't exactly know the provisions of my dowry."

He shook his head. "Perhaps you should find that out before you offer yourself to a man...any man."

She cocked her head to the side as she looked at him. "Any man? I'd never ask another besides you."

Fuck. Didn't she know what words like that did to a man? To know she wanted him alone or perhaps that she trusted only him. He was so tempted...

He ought not to be. She only wanted a single night from him. Not that he wanted marriage, either, but it was the principle of the matter. He'd been a rich woman's plaything more than once and he'd not allow himself to be so again.

Still. He let go of her braid and the hair had once again curled around the lush curve of her breast. "You seem so slender..."

"What's that?" she asked, confusion clouding her gaze.

He closed the distance between them, wrapping an arm under her backside as he lifted her to his chest.

Her hands twined about his neck as her legs came about his waist.

Those breasts crushed against him and he held both her ass cheeks in his palms. He nearly lost his faculties because her ass was as round and lush as her chest. The plump flesh filled his hands, her apex settled against the hard ridge of his cock.

"Do you want to know what you're asking of me? What it might be like?"

She gasped then. "You're going to actually ruin me? Here? Now?"

He looked down at her, drowning in the green of her eyes. There was some fear but also curiosity and desire lurking in their depths. "No. I won't take your maidenhead. Though, even kissing you today was..." Foolish. That was the word that came to mind.

"Wonderful," she sighed, tightening her legs about him.

A man could only take so much. Here was a woman who made him ache. And even though she only wanted him for what every other woman seemed to want him for, he knew that she was special. To him.

Climbing up the bank, he lowered his mouth to hers. This time, the kiss wasn't gentle. Hot want coursed through him, and he kissed her with all the passion he possessed. The kiss was hard, intense, powerful as he parted her lips and plundered her mouth with his tongue.

But she didn't frighten. Emma never did. Instead, she moaned into his mouth, locked her legs about him, and kissed him back, her tongue thrusting against his as her hips rolled into him.

He dropped to his knees, heedless of the pain that shot through his exhausted legs, kneading her ass as he helped her rub up and down the length of his cock.

Their tongues tangled all the more as she crashed against him, panting into his mouth.

It was hard and fast and so fucking perfect that he had to keep from yanking down his breeches and doing the very thing he'd just said he wouldn't do, take her maidenhead.

But by some miracle, he kept his wits as one of his hands skated up her side and wedged between their bodies to give one of her breasts a firm squeeze.

Being with her, touching her, was everything he'd dreamed it would be. She was so soft, and lush, and full, and so perfect that a moan ripped from his lips as she arched into his caress, her nipple hardening against his palm.

"Emma," he gritted out, lying her down in the grass so that his cock pressed even more deeply between her thighs.

She had twisted her fingers into his hair, and she pulled at the strands, mixing a bit of pain into the pleasure in the most satisfying way. Her heels had come to his backside, and they dug into his flesh, urging him closer.

Their embrace felt like an explosion of passion, as though a dam had given way, unleashing a torrent of feelings.

He shifted his hand to drag the pad of his thumb across her nipple, growling out his satisfaction as the pebble of skin further stiffened and she cried into his mouth.

No woman had ever felt more like his in his arms. He shook off the thought, sure that it would recede with the passion, but as she panted underneath him, wrapped all about him, he wasn't certain he wanted this moment to end.

And then she broke apart, her cry echoing into the night.

He'd not planned it, but his own finish came roaring over him, his seed spilling into the soaking breeches he still wore.

But he didn't let her go. In fact, he held her close for the longest time, continuing to kiss her with long, languid kisses as his heartbeat slowly returned to normal, but damn him to hell because while the passion had receded, the feelings did not.

What was he going to do with them? He had a plan. And Miss Emma Blake was everything he'd sworn he did *not* want.

CHAPTER TEN

TRISTON ATTEMPTED to sleep that night, he truly did. His body was beyond exhausted after multiple fights and a lengthy soak in cold water.

Not to mention the release. He'd not even been inside Emma, and yet the experience had been one of the best in his life.

She'd been so responsive in his arms and so perfect...well...for him. It hadn't been soft, he wasn't a soft man.

But she'd matched his passion. It wasn't until he lay in bed alone that he realized how rare an experience that had been throughout his life.

And then there was her heart. It was larger than her breasts, which was rather miraculous.

Rising before the sun, he dressed, determined to return to London before anyone expected him. With the meeting still two days away, Guiltmore and his lackies would be expecting him to travel tomorrow. Or at least he hoped so.

He didn't take his phaeton. Instead, he had one of Rush's horses saddled and set out at a good clip. If he only stopped when necessary, he'd make it to London by late afternoon.

He remained vigilant, but no one attempted to give him trouble on the road except for an overloaded farmer's cart and one carriage with two gawking ladies. Both were attractive enough, he'd guess sisters, but he could not have been less interested.

As he rode, his thoughts settled on Emma over and over, considering what it might mean to change his path, to actually contemplate a future with a woman.

He swiped a hand over his brow. He'd have to give up his dream to own a boxing club.

He'd not spend Emma's money on her care, even if he received it. And he'd need every penny he'd saved to buy a respectable home.

Perhaps in a few years he'd be able to save enough to try again. He could still train. Maybe even take on a few fighters like Winter in order to start his business on the side until he could open a club of his own.

But he frowned.

Emma didn't seem all that interested in the trimmings of the fine life, but he'd keep her in a decent life. She'd need a cook and at least one maid.

He blew out a breath as he neared London, moved into a steady stream of carriages and horses waiting to cross the North Bridge.

By the time he reached his family home in Cheapside, exhaustion pulled at his limbs, but he settled the horse in the small stable at the back of the alley and made his way in through the kitchen.

At the click of the door, a woman he didn't recognize turned from the stove and let out a blood-curdling scream at the sight of him.

She was a little lady with grey hair, and he could hardly imagine how she managed to make that much noise, but he didn't ask because feet thundered down the stairs, both Gris and Fulton appearing in the kitchen.

"It's you," Gris roared, crossing the room and slapping him on the back. "What are you doing here? Rush's letter only just arrived."

"Missus Mable," Fulton turned to the woman at the stove. "You can cease your banshee scream. This is our brother, Lord Triston."

"Saint Lucifer, you frightened me," the woman said, dropping the wooden spoon she'd been holding up. Had she meant to use that as a weapon against him? Hilarious.

"My apologies for entering my own home," he said and then turned to his brothers. "Care to explain who Missus Mable is and why she is here?"

Gris shrugged. "With our schedule at Hell's Corner we decided we needed someone to cook."

"And clean a bit," Fulton added, crossing his arms over his chest as though he were daring Triston to argue. Fulton was smaller than Tris but a scrappy fighter. As a smuggler, he did his share of tussling.

"I see." Triston knew the club had been flush with money, but his brothers were hiring servants?

Fulton's body had relaxed, and he gave his brother a wink. "We've got your cut and Rush's too. We'll save Ace's for when he returns from his northern estate."

"You saved my cut? Even though I haven't been working?" he asked, surprised and pleased it had occurred to his brothers.

"You've been working." Gris waved his hand. "Sounds like you got the shittiest job of all having to meet with this lawyer. Is it true they attacked your woman?"

"My woman?" he barked, not ready for more of his brothers to ask about Emma. He hardly knew how he felt without them poking at him.

"Rush said something about her defending you," Fulton added with a derisive chuckle. "You're slipping, big brother."

Gris gave Fulton a hard shove, sending him crashing into the prep table in the center of the kitchen. "Shut it."

Fulton straightened up and barreled at Gris, getting ready for a full-on brawl. This was what Tris expected from his brothers.

He stepped in front of Gris, giving Fulton just enough room to think he might sidestep Tris, and then he locked an arm about his little brother's neck, spinning him in another direction. "Focus." He thumped a hand on Fulton's back.

Fulton pushed against his chest, breaking free, but he didn't charge at Gris again.

"So, she's not your woman?" Gris asked, leaning against the door frame. "Because Rush also said something about her being a beauty."

"What's it to you?" Raw jealousy shot through him. No one was touching Emma but him.

"Well." Gris looked up at the ceiling. "I'll be visiting Rush soon. Might be I'd like a bit of company while I'm out in the country."

He punched the heel of his hand against Gris's chest with all the force he had, and Gris flew back out of the kitchen, crashing into the wall on the far side of the hall.

"How come you get to hit him and I don't?"

"Out of the kitchen," Mrs. Mable called. "Before you ruin dinner."

Fulton started to shuffle out, but Tris arched his brows. "You listen to the cook?"

Fulton shrugged. "She makes the best meat pie you've ever tasted."

Tris shook his head. His brothers had been staunchly against servants. They were the trappings of aristocracy. What was happening to his family?

"I know what you're thinking," Gris said, dusting himself off. Shoving each other was part of the daily conversation in their house. "But with just the two of us, we didn't have time to run the club, ship the wine, make the gin, and cook regular meals."

He gave a nod. Things were changing. There was no denying that. "Can one of you join me to attend this soirée with Guiltmore tomorrow night?"

"Soirée?" Fulton snorted. "The fucking French."

Gris laughed too. "You got it, big brother. I'm there. Fulton's back in town for a few days anyhow, he can take care of Hell's Corner tomorrow night."

Fulton gave a nod. "Rush mentioned inviting East too."

Tris sighed. "I'm going to go see him tonight. Rush thinks he can help..."

"He's an earl—they're all shit," Fulton rumbled.

"Even our father?" Tris asked, though he knew the answer.

Gris snorted as they all started up the stairs. "Especially our late father."

He ran a tired hand through his hair. He already missed the country air. He'd never wanted to live in the countryside, but he'd like to have his feet in the river right now, with a lovely derriere resting in his lap. Emma's, to be exact.

Derriere. That was the perfect word for Emma's backside. The French had gotten a few words just right.

———

EMMA MANAGED to milk her sore ankle for a few more days of bedrest, but by Friday, her mother had grown too impatient for Emma to make her confinement last another day.

She rose from the bed, dressed, and made her way downstairs to break her fast. Her mother arrived a half hour later, seating herself at the head of the table.

"Lady Smith will be arriving during your calling hours," her mother said as she picked up her fork.

"How wonderful." Emma lifted her brows, surprised that something pleasant had come from leaving her room.

"And tomorrow," her mother added, her voice turning to steel, "you'll go on a carriage ride with Lord Marsden."

Her stomach dropped and a sick feeling climbed into the back of her throat. "Mother. No."

"I don't know what your issue is with the man but—"

"He isn't nice. He's cruel and—" She tried to get the words out before her mother interrupted her.

"Stop," her mother said, loudly enough to silence Emma's protest.

Emma felt tears welling in her eyes. She needed to be heard. Understood. "Please."

"You think your father was my first choice?" her mother asked, the words tearing at something inside. Emma had never heard her mother talk like this and she didn't wish to now. "He was not the man I wanted to marry."

Drawing in a deep breath, Emma tried to think rationally. "I'm not concerned about a love match." She was. She could see that now. She'd not wanted to wed because she didn't want to be forced into a relationship with a man who didn't like or respect her. But she needed her mother to understand. "But father had a kind heart and a gentle way about him. Lord Marsden has neither."

Her mother waved her hand. "Spoiled children. That's what his kindness brought. Look at you—willful and disobedient. If he'd had a spine…"

Emma's jaw clenched. She'd not listen to this diatribe against her father. "He made me feel like an actual person. Like I mattered. Like my needs and my dreams mattered. Not just a doll to be trussed up and waved in front of a man with a title."

Her mother's fork clattered on the table. "You'll do your duty to this family, and you'll allow Marsden to court you."

"I won't," she cried, her spine stiffening. She never spoke like this to her mother, but something inside her shifted. She was important, at least to a few. It wasn't only her father who found her worthy, Tristan did too. And that mattered.

But her newfound strength was short-lived. "You think Natalie can have a season if you don't? If you won't think of me, think of her," her mother said, her eyes narrowing into fine points of triumph.

Emma's defiance deflated like the bladder of a pig. She hardly held back the tears as her mother rose from the table once again. She knew she'd won.

"Enjoy your visit with Lady Smith today. I've extended Lord Marsden's visit. You will allow him to court you, and no more of your shenanigans." And then she swept out of the room.

Long after her mother had gone, Emma sat staring at nothing in particular, wondering what she was to do.

She thought of Tris and how he'd made her promise that she'd come to him. Her chest ached because she'd not seen him in a few days, but even if he could help her, what was to be done about Natalie?

Her mother was correct. Without proper financing, Natalie would not have a season. Would her uncle not provide that? Did she ask him? He'd returned home after the ball, but he only lived a few villages away. The ride could be done in a few hours. Should she see him? Write to him?

And could Emma stomach a life with Marsden for Natalie's sake? Her insides twisted and churned at the idea. The rest of her food forgotten, she rose and moved to the salon where she waited for Abby to arrive.

She didn't need to wait long. Abby arrived within a quarter hour, her smile lighting the room despite Emma's glum mood.

"I'm so glad to see you're well," Abby cried as Emma rose to embrace her.

Her smile grew thin, but she kept it on her lips as they sat down.

"I'm so glad you're here," Emma said.

"As am I," Abby said, taking one of Emma's hands. "Though I should confess that I am here at Lord Triston's request."

Her heart rose into her throat. She'd missed Triston the last few days. She hadn't bothered to sneak out again, since she'd assumed he'd gone to London. "Do you know how he fares?"

Abby shook her head. "No. But Rush asked their brothers to help him, so I'm sure he's safe."

Emma looked down at her lap, her fingers twisting together.

"Thank you for helping him the other day."

She appreciated the sentiment. "I hardly did a thing. Truly."

Abby shook her head. "That isn't true. Triston will help anyone in need, but I know him better than anyone else in Rush's family, besides Rush, of course." Abby grinned at the mention of her husband. "But I can tell you that he never allows people to give him aid. The fact that you did, I know it matters."

Emma wasn't sure that it did. Even if Tris liked her more for her actions, that wouldn't save Emma from her mother's plans, from what Emma needed to do for her sister.

"Do you know when he'll be back?" Emma asked, knowing that she'd need to explain to him. She wasn't certain why. There was no promise between them. But she'd asked him to help her in a way. Ruin her, to be specific, and she now understood that she couldn't be so rash. She'd have to bear her responsibility for her sister's sake.

74

CHAPTER ELEVEN

THE NEXT NIGHT, East stood on one side of Tris, with Gris on the other. His half-brother and his full brother had not met and, if the current silence was any indication, it should have stayed like that.

They'd done nothing but growl at one another.

Still…Tris was glad to have both men with him. East was a strong man with social and political sway, and Gris, thanks to his gin, had the allegiance of many a criminal tucked in his back pocket.

"East," Tris said as they stood in the shadows across from the loading dock. Men hauled crates from a ship and called to one another, making plenty of noise, allowing Tris to speak freely to both his brothers. They'd hidden themselves away to survey the scene but thus far, nothing seemed amiss.

"Yes?" East asked.

"What's happened with the Den of Sins?" A muscle in his jaw ticced as he waited for the answer. The other gaming hell had been bought by Guiltmore, but because the man had used a false name, the sale had become null and void.

"We're still looking for another buyer. I asked Ace about purchasing the club, but he's had his hands full."

Tris shifted, twisting his neck until it gave a definite crack. "I've been thinking…"

"About what?" Gris asked, turning toward him.

"We should purchase it. Fold it into our business."

"Why?" Gris asked. "We're hardly covering Hell's Corner as it is."

"I'll come back. But two clubs would make twice the profit and—"

Gris interrupted. "And twice the headache."

Tris grimaced. "Not necessarily. The more clubs we own, the less of a threat Guiltmore poses. As a single shop, we're just a nuisance to his business, but if we owned more, we'd be a force."

"Or a bigger target," Gris fired back.

East scratched his chin. "Money can buy you more protection. The more you make, the more insulated you'll be."

"Exactly," Tris answered.

"Fuck that." Gris spat on the ground. "I can barely manage with just the one club. I want more freedom, not less."

Tris grimaced. He'd felt that same way not a week prior. But now he needed to make money. If he was even going to consider a life with a woman like Emma… And he was considering that very thing. He knew that now.

"Can you find out the sale price for me?" Tris asked, ignoring Gris.

Gris opened his mouth to argue further, but four men approached the docks. Their long coats flapped in the breeze as they moved, and the dock workers disappeared at the sight of them.

"Here we go," East said, then turned to Gris. "Would you canvas behind us and keep an eye out from the shadows in case it's a trap?"

To Tris's astonishment, Gris didn't argue. He gave a brisk nod and then melted into the darkness.

He and East stepped out, moving toward the lanterns that swung near the now-abandoned boat.

"Well, hello," one man called. Shorter than the others, he had all the markers of a middle-aged solicitor, from the bowler perched on his head to his expanding waistline.

"Guiltmore?" Tris asked, his arms crossing.

"Guilty," the man chuckled at his own joke.

He didn't respond as he waited for the man to continue. The silence stretched on until Guiltmore finally cleared his throat. "You must be wondering why I've called you here."

Still Tris didn't say a word. If there was one thing he was good at, it was intimidating with a frown alone. Of course, if that failed, there were his fists...

Guiltmore shifted as the three men behind him attempted to look menacing. Tris's hand passed over the loaded pistol in his breast pocket.

"Your brother has been very resistant to our negotiations."

"And I look more flexible to you?" he asked, actually smirking.

"No, but I know you've made real estate inquiries into properties for sale. Places far better suited to a boxing club than a gaming hell."

Tris swore softly to himself. That's why they'd come to him. They saw him as the weak link in the family business.

He'd rot in prison or hell before he sold out his family. He heard East suck in a quick breath.

"Tell him it's useless," one of the men in the back said. "Tell him Gyla already has—"

"Commander," Guiltmore bit out, his voice hard. "That is enough."

Gyla? He looked at East, whose gaze had narrowed into slits. "So, you're the Commander?"

Another of the men pulled out a pistol, and Tris shoved East to the side, pulling out his own gun.

An explosion of powder filled the air and Tris crouched as he pulled the hammer back. But as the smoke cleared, it wasn't him or East who was harmed.

The man they called Commander lay dead on the ground.

"You shot your own man?" Tris asked, taking a step back as East pulled himself from the ground, coming to Triston's side once again.

"He talked too much," Guiltmore said with a shrug.

"Or you just didn't need him any longer since you've procured both his clubs," East fired back.

"Oh, but you needn't worry about that, Lord Easton," Guiltmore said smoothly. "Our boss has a respect for the peerage, being of noble descent himself."

"Gyla?" Tris asked.

Guiltmore waved his hand. "He prefers to remain anonymous, but you can be assured that I speak for him and that his pockets are deep enough to buy both Hell's Corner and renegotiate the Den of Sins."

Triston blew out a breath, his pistol still firmly tucked in his hand. "Tell him that we appreciate his offer, but that neither club is for sale."

Guiltmore clicked his tongue. "You're making a big mistake."

East's hand came to his shoulder, pulling him back. Triston did as his brother asked, slowly backing up to where Gris waited in the shadows.

"Our next meeting will not be so friendly," Guiltmore called. "We can make you rich men."

Tris's lip curled as he stopped moving. "I need you to understand, Guiltmore, that I am a relentless fighter. Don't provoke my ire."

Guiltmore paused. "Our boss isn't afraid of a man like—"

Tris raised his pistol. "I'm not talking to him. I'm talking to you. Threaten me again, and you'll know what it feels like to have a pugilist knock in your teeth."

Guiltmore took a half step back and Triston used that hesitation to disappear in the shadows.

Not that he was running. If anything, his path had been cemented. He was going to marry Emma, provide a wonderful life for her with his family's business. And as for Guiltmore and Gyla? They'd soon learn that Triston was a man who was made for the fight.

———

THE NEXT DAY, Emma sat beside Marsden attempting not to fidget. They rode along the country lane, saying little as the crisp fall breeze pulled at her bonnet ribbons.

She was glad for the coolness, wearing a heavy velvet riding habit that she hoped would act like armor.

He'd driven with a speed that had her grasping at the side of his phaeton, doing her best not to bounce into him or touch him in any way at all, and she'd been mostly successful.

Now they were rounding a bend in a road that would lead home in just a short quarter hour and she could almost taste freedom. She'd done it. She'd survived an outing with Lord Marsden.

Marsden slowed down as they approached a pair of large willows that skirted the country lane.

She let out a rush of air, relieved not to be speeding so quickly down the bumpy roads, until the carriage drew to a stop.

What was he doing?

But as he turned to her, holding the reins in a single hand, she winced, knowing she'd take speed over his undivided attention any day.

"Miss Blake," he said, his hand reaching for hers.

Unwittingly, she pulled her own back. "Yes?"

"You don't like me."

She blinked in surprise. "My lord?" She didn't like him. Not even a little, but him asking that made her wildly uncomfortable.

"I made a bad impression that first night when I kissed you."

Kissing? It had been a full-on attack.

"My apologies. I thought that you would welcome..." He trailed off. "I'd like to start over."

Her shoulders slumped as she thought of her sister and her mother's words. "Start over?"

"Yes," he said. "Shall we walk? The air is lovely this time of year."

"It is, but we've gotten a fair bit of it. Are you certain you wouldn't rather return to the house for tea?" For once, she'd prefer her mother's watchful eye.

"I have noticed that you like to be outside."

That was nice, to have noticed her preference. Taking in a big gulp of air, she nodded her consent as he stepped down from the small carriage to come around and help her down as well. She fought the urge to pick up the reins and drive off, and instead, placed her hand in his and then allowed him to help her out.

"Those trees are impressive," he murmured. "Shall we look at them?"

"All right," she replied, giving him a sidelong glance. They were common willows. Why would he wish to look at them?

But they'd no more rounded the trunk than he pulled her a touch closer. "You see, Emma, they are so tall because they have grown roots together. If one came down, the other would follow."

"That is lovely, actually," she said, enjoying his company the slightest bit. He stopped, under the canopy of branches.

"And you see," he said, staring down at her, his face unreadable, "I have no intention of having a wife who wants separate roots from me."

She cocked her head, sensing the dark turn they'd just taken. "I don't know what you mean—"

His other hand shot out, gripping her upper arm. "You're a beautiful woman."

She didn't answer as she tried to tug away.

"But I expect obedience in a bride, and during my stay you've proven every rumor about your wayward behavior true."

She gasped in a breath as he kept pulling. "Then find another lady."

"Oh, but..." he said, then he gave her the sort of grin that turned her blood cold. "I like a challenge."

She screamed then, even as he gave her hard shove. Tumbling to the ground, she attempted to scramble away, but he was on top of her before she could get far.

He grabbed at her arms, and though she attempted to twist away, somehow, he managed to subdue her, his body pressing hers, his breath hot and rank in her face.

She turned away a moment before he kissed her, which meant that he began lapping at her neck with his lips and tongue.

She cried out even as he let go of her arm to palm her breast.

His touch was hard and painful, nothing like Triston's. Fear and revulsion threatened to engulf her as she tried to use her free hand to uselessly push him away. And then, twisting, she saw the rock. It was palm-sized, and her hand reached out—stretching, she grasped the stone, bringing down with all the force she could muster, right into his temple.

He slumped on top of her, and she didn't bother to wonder how badly he was hurt as she pushed him to the side and then bolted up.

Lifting her skirts, she blindly ran.

CHAPTER TWELVE

TRISTON HAD ALMOST MADE it to Upton Falls when the rain began to fall. Light at first, but by the time he was nearing his brother's home, it poured down with a driving force that soaked through his clothes. Which was how he nearly missed the crumpled pile of garments in the cemetery on the border of his brother's land.

At least he thought it was a pile of clothing. What else would be on the ground in this sort of weather?

Just in front of a headstone, he squinted, attempting to decide why a lump of fabric would be there.

But as he swiped water from his eyes, he realized that the clothing had a person inside it.

"Hey," he called out. "Are you all right?"

He received no answer. But the bundle moved, an arm raising up a bit before sinking back to the ground. A very slender arm...

Pulling up his horse, he swung down.

He'd only slept a few hours before he'd started back for Rush's home. He'd told Gris and Fulton that he wanted to update Rush, but the truth was...he'd missed Emma.

He wanted to hold her in his arms, know that she was safe, and start making real plans for their future.

As he stomped through several puddles, he tried again. "Hello," he called. "Are you hurt?"

The person turned toward him, and his heart nearly ceased beating in his chest. Emma.

Her face was nearly devoid of color, her lips purple, and her eyes... vacant. They held no sparkle.

Suddenly he was running, shucking his coat and scooping her up in his arms, wrapping her in the heavy garment.

He swung up on the horse, holding her against his body as he nudged the animal forward. He knew the gelding was tired after a long day, but he had all he could do not to send the beast into a gallop.

"Emma?" he ground out. "What's wrong?"

She blinked up at him, her pupils dilated, and she mumbled, "Cold."

"Why were you lying on the ground? Did someone hurt you?"

And that's when he saw her mouth tighten.

Fuck. Who had hurt her? He'd kill whoever had done this. His first thought was Guiltmore. He'd already planned to make that man pay, but if he'd touched Emma, he'd torch that man and everything he loved to the ground.

"Tell me."

"Marsden," she whispered. "He..."

Rage roared through him, swift and fierce. He was going to kill him. Slowly and painfully.

They reached the house and he climbed off the horse, giving its backside a slap to send it to the stables. A groom would see the beast cared for.

He bolted up the stairs, throwing open the door and barking out several commands. "Hot water. Warm blankets. Broth. Now!"

And then he took the stairs two at a time, entering his own chamber as he unceremoniously began stripping off Emma's wet clothing, leaving only her chemise.

He didn't look. Not really. He did note that there was no blood and very little bruising. And when he had her wrapped in the coverlet of his bed, he stripped off his own soaked clothing until he wore nothing but his breeches.

The butler arrived with two mugs of steaming broth and said nothing about Emma wrapped in blankets on Triston's bed. "The water will be up in just a moment, my lord."

Tris only nodded as he strode over with the broth. Lifting Emma onto his lap, he sat down again and brought the warm liquid to her lips.

She took several sips and then a swallow, some of the color returning to her cheeks. "Oh. That's better."

"Good. Now tell me how badly he hurt you so I know how long it should take me to murder him."

She was almost completely covered in blankets, only her face peeking out, which somehow made her smile even more beautiful. "You'd murder him for me?"

"Oh, sweetheart," he whispered, placing a light kiss on the tip of her nose. "I'd enjoy murdering him. You should know, I'd do far worse for you."

Her eyes went wide as her lips parted in invitation—one he didn't take, though he badly wanted to.

"You would?" She tried to sit up a little then, but he pulled her closer to his chest, his lips grazing her temple.

"Now tell me, love. I want to know. What happened?"

"He pushed me to the ground and then…" She looked away, color draining from her face all over again.

Outwardly, he remained calm, but inwardly, the fighter raged to the surface, ready to go to battle for her.

He should have been there. He was determined to remain by his family's side. It was in their best interest and provided him the greatest chance to care for Emma. But he'd never leave her again. Not defenseless like that.

"And then what happened?"

"He tried to kiss me and touch me and then I grabbed a rock and…"

Interesting. "And then what?"

"I bashed him in the head."

The air rushed from his lungs. "You did?"

"I did." That garnered a bit of a smile as she snuggled in deeper to his lap. "I knocked him out too." Then her brow knitted. "You don't think I killed him, do you?"

"If you did, good riddance."

"Triston," she cried, sitting up this time. The blanket slid down one shoulder, revealing creamy skin. "What if I did? Would they send me to prison?"

"Emma," he whispered, and this time he kissed her lips. "I would never allow anyone to do that. We'd leave the country first."

"We?" she asked, and then, cocking her head, she added, "Where?"

———

EMMA WONDERED if the cold had truly seeped into her brain. She'd been so upset after Marsden's attack that when she'd mindlessly run, she'd found herself in front of her father's grave.

Lying down, she'd attempted to ask him what she ought to do. Of course, he hadn't answered. But she'd begged him to send her a sign. She'd not wish to abandon Natalie, but was she to marry the cruel Marsden in order to secure her sister's future? Her mother's? Was that her path? Her only option?

Her answer had come first as rain and then as Triston, scooping her up into his arms and stripping her down to her chemise.

Was that the sign she'd waited for?

"What country could we run away to? I don't know." He looked up at the ceiling seeming to contemplate. "Where would you wish to go? My brother Fulton makes regular stops in both France and Italy. Do you fancy wine?"

"Wine?"

He nodded. "I was going to purchase another gaming hell. Start a second club to provide for us, but if we had to flee the country, we

TAMMY ANDRESEN

could purchase a winery instead. I bet my brothers would buy our wine for their club."

His words washed over her. "Our wine? Our vineyard?"

He paused, looking up at the ceiling. "Right. I just assumed you'd rather run away with me than go to prison, but perhaps…"

"Triston," she admonished, pulling one hand from the blanket and touching his face. "Tris. Why would you even say such a thing. Of course I would. I just thought that you weren't all that enamored of me."

"Emma," he said, then let out a long breath as he stroked her hair back from her face. The door opened and the metal tub was dragged in and then bucket after bucket of water was dumped in, filling it up.

As the room emptied again, he stood with her in his arms and then murmured close to her ear. "I'll turn my back while you get in the tub."

"All right," she answered as he lightly set her on her feet.

She tried to keep her hands steady, knowing she was stripping naked with him in the room. But between the cold and his presence, she could hardly remove the clothing. She finally managed to pull the garment over her head and sank into the water. Grabbing the cake of soap, she quickly scrubbed her body.

When she was done, she looked over to see his bare back, muscles rippling as he crossed his arms. He was still turned away. "I'm nearly done."

"I would like to say, just to be clear, that I've always been enamored with you." He didn't look over his shoulder at her, but the words still hit her square in the chest.

Her heart rose into her throat and she sat up in the water. "I'm not certain I believe you."

He half looked over his shoulder and she sank down again, hiding behind the high walls of the tub.

"I mentioned to you once that you weren't the first high-born woman that I've been acquainted with. You are, in fact, the third."

Emma hardly knew what to say so she just let him continue, though the blood rushed in her ears as her heart continued to pound.

"The first was a woman very much like you. Young, a debutante. I was acquainted with her brother and the very first moment we met, the attraction was undeniable."

The words pulled at her chest, jealousy twisting in her stomach. "I see."

He quirked a small smile. "I was a gentleman, by the way. But when I asked permission to court, not only was I denied, but I was also escorted out of their home at the end of a pistol."

"Oh," she gasped. "That is terrible."

"She married a baron a very short time later." He ran a hand through his hair. "Refused to see me after she'd been forbidden to by her parents."

Emma winced. "It's not her fault. The pressure from family to marry well can be overwhelming."

"You are resisting."

She shook her head. "I'm trying but not always succeeding."

He turned to her then, his body straight and strong. "What do you mean?"

She sighed. She'd tell Triston the truth. Always. She could be impulsive, but she'd not be dishonest. "My mother told me that I was not only ruining myself, but I was also destroying Natalie's chances of a good match by denying Marsden. I..."

"That's why you were with him today?"

"Yes."

Triston crossed to the tub, squatting down so their eyes were near level, only the side of the tub between them. She tried to keep the heat from crawling up her face as she stared into his dark eyes.

One hand came to her cheek and he cupped her face in his palm. "You're a good person for wanting to care for your sister."

"Despite wanting to do the right thing, I'm not succeeding, at least where Natalie is concerned. And the question I keep asking myself is, am I doing my usual job of mucking everything up by being here?"

Triston's head whipped back like she'd slapped him.

She winced, rising higher in the tub and forgetting all about her nudity.

"You think being with him is right?" The snarl in his voice told her that she'd made a mistake. But how did she explain?

CHAPTER THIRTEEN

TRISTON TRIED to calm the raging thud of his heart against his chest. Despite all he'd decided, all he'd be willing to give Emma, she still saw him as an error in judgment.

Why did he open himself up for this sort of hurt over and over? Why hadn't he learned?

But then Emma rose out of the water, standing in the tub completely naked, water streaming down her body. He couldn't help himself as he stared at every inch. From her large, round breasts to her tiny waist, down the flat of her stomach to the triangle of auburn hair at her apex.

He stood too, want coursing through him even as he cursed himself.

"Tell me about the other woman."

"What?"

"The second woman," she said with a frown.

Hurt as he was, angry at her, even, he still worried about her comfort. She'd grow cold again… "Come out of there and wrap up."

She reached for his hand then, using him to balance as she stepped out of the tub, coming to stand right in front of him. His other hand itched to pull her even closer.

Instead, he let go of her, picked up the blanket, and wrapped it around her shoulders.

Then he shucked his breeches and stepped into the tub. He heard her sharp intake of breath and a bit of satisfaction coursed through him. If she were going to reject him as a mistake, she ought to know what she was giving up.

But as he sank into the warm water, her fingers threaded into his hair, lightly massaging his scalp. She sank down next to him on the other side of the tub.

Her touch relaxed him far more than it ought, which was likely why he found himself saying, "She was a countess."

"Widowed or married?"

"Married," he grunted, his eyes squeezing shut. "I know. It was foolish, but she was in London, he was at their country estate. They'd been apart for months. I thought they had a marriage in name only."

"What happened?"

Why did he keep confessing to her? But the words tumbled from his lips anyway. "The earl found out, came to London, and attempted to have me tossed in prison. I fled the country and they reunited. Apparently, his zeal in chasing me off renewed her interest."

Her lips grazed his temple. "Triston, you are also afraid of making the same mistake with me that you've made in the past."

His eyes flew open as he realized that was true.

"And I understand now that your hesitation when you first met me was not about me at all but about your own past."

He turned to look at her, realization making his chest tight. "And yours is not about me either."

She shook her head. "You are wonderful. Strong, caring, beyond what I even imagined. It's my own selfishness I'm worried about. Do I want you at the expense of my sister?"

He understood and it was his turn to rise from the water. Not bothering to dry off, he stepped out and pulled her against him. "Emma."

"Tell me I can still see my sister well married even if we wed and I won't hesitate again, but I don't trust my own judgment. It's been so long since I feel as though I made the right choice."

He gathered her into his arms. It was time to tell her everything. "Emma," he started as her bare arms wrapped about his neck, pulling the blanket over his shoulders too, "I need you to know that I'd—" He stopped, just before the bed. "I will do whatever it takes to provide for you. I can't say that I'm the right choice. Perhaps that's why I grow so offended when you question your choices, because I worry that I've never been good enough for you."

She blinked several times. "Triston." She reached for his face, her green eyes holding his captive. "If one of us isn't good enough, it's not you. It's never been you."

Something deep rumbled in his chest. He was rewriting his entire life for this woman. Didn't she understand? "You are wrong, Emma. You're a goddess among women. There isn't anything I wouldn't do to make you mine."

She stared down at him, attempting to process those words. "You don't mean that."

"I do mean that. Every word." He wouldn't burden her with his plans for the club, how he was considering buying the Den of Sins to provide for her. But he'd come to realize that his responsibilities to her, to his family, were what was most important in life.

She stared at him as though searching for what to say, but words were not what he needed now.

Closing the distance between their mouths, he took her lips with his.

Her lips pressed to his with a warm intimacy that made him not only want her more, but somehow reaffirmed every feeling he'd had.

She was his to hold and to protect.

———

EMMA TRIED to reconcile the man she'd first met with the one who was kissing her as though she were the most precious thing in the world.

91

Triston was larger than life. Untouchable and unbreachable, except that right now she was in nothing but a blanket and he wore nothing at all. Now he held her in his arms, softly kissing her, as he told her that nothing was more important to him than her.

The rightness of being here with him settled over her like another warm blanket.

With clarity, she knew she was in the right place. She didn't want to be a debutante or spend her time with earls like Marsden. She much preferred plain-speaking, honest, and strong lords who offered to run away to Italy with her.

She smiled against his mouth.

"What's funny?" he asked, pulling back a bit.

"Nothing. Just…what do you think Italians will think of my red hair? You'd blend right in, but me…"

His brows shot up for a moment before he laughed. "They'll likely think what I do—that you are gorgeously exotic."

A blush was surely staining her cheeks as heat filled them.

"Of course, I've also been wondering what color hair you had about your womanhood and—"

"Triston," she gasped, giving his shoulders a smack. "You did not think about that. Did you?"

He let out a low rumble of laughter, sexy and intimate and so male. "I did. Often."

She'd seen him too, every powerful inch of him, and she had to confess, she was also eager to see more. Study the hard planes of his body, trace his muscles. She did so now, feeling the thick, corded bulge of his shoulders and then down his biceps as he kissed her again. On and on she traced, down his back and up his sides until their kiss grew heated, their tongues tangling together.

And then she pulled back. "Triston?"

"Yes?"

His eyes were dark and his breath heavy as he looked at her. It was so sexy that she nearly forgot her question.

But she was a lady, and she had asked him in the past if he'd ruin her and so she needed to ask now. "Are we...are we going to ruin me now? Or..."

His mouth set in that frown, the one she was accustomed to seeing. "Ruin you?" Slowly he lay her on the bed, his weight coming down on her. The blanket still separated them, but she wished to feel his skin. "If you'll have me, Emma, I mean to make you my wife."

That stilled her heart. And rather than answer, she lifted up to kiss him again. Her fingers threaded into his hair as she tugged him closer.

She wanted all of him. Every massive inch.

He tugged at the edge of the blanket, slowly removing the cloth from between them until his bare chest pressed to hers.

And then he stopped kissing her mouth to instead blaze a trail along her jaw, down her neck, and over her chest. And when his tongue flicked out over one of her nipples, pleasure coursed through her.

She moaned as she skimmed her hands over his shoulders again. And then he sucked her puckered flesh between his lips, his tongue sweeping over the sensitive nub until she writhed in pleasure under him.

She never wanted him to stop.

"Triston," Rush's muffled voice called out from the other side of the door. "I need to speak with you."

"Not now." Triston did not lift his head, instead he rested his cheek in the valley between her breasts.

"Yes. Now."

"Rush." Triston blew out a breath, tickling her skin.

"Right now," his brother responded. "You come out or I'm coming in."

"All right," he answered with a scowl. But his look softened when his eyes met hers. Triston lifted himself up and tucked the blanket around her before he stood and crossed the room to the wardrobe to pull out a fresh pair of breeches.

She watched him, marveling once again at his body and the strength there. "Is everything all right?"

He looked back at her, starting across the room again, not even bothering with a shirt. "It will all be fine, love. You stay warm and I'll be back in just a minute." Then he leaned over and kissed her forehead before he left the room.

CHAPTER FOURTEEN

TRIS STEPPED out into the hall, knowing what he'd find.

Rush took a healthy swing at him, and he only just stepped out of the way of the fist. "Really? You're going to hit a boxer?"

He'd yet to even close the door and he heard Emma gasp. "Tris?"

"It's all right, sweetheart." He gently closed the door, scowling at his brother. "Now you've gone and worried her."

Rush poked him hard in the bare chest. "We're going to discuss my wrongdoing here?"

That was a reasonable point. "I haven't done anything wrong." Perhaps that was a bit of a stretch. He had stripped her naked and he'd just been fondling her bare breasts. But somehow, he couldn't bring himself to regret either action.

"You've ruined her," Rush hissed. "In my house."

"I'm going to marry her, Rush." The simple truth seemed the easiest solution.

His brother froze, staring at him. Then a small smile tugged at his lips. "I knew it."

He'd like to deny it, but his brother likely had realized what was happening before Tris did himself. "There is no need to gloat. I don't have the best record with members of the peerage, and it took me a bit to understand she wouldn't hurt me as the rest have."

"Even our father," Rush said, his voice dropped to a menacing level as he scowled. "How could we trust any of them after the way he treated us?"

Triston nodded, sure his brother was right.

"But," Rush went on, "she can't be here, Tris. Her family is our neighbor. You must take her home and make up some excuse."

"I won't," he growled out so furiously that even Rush took a step back.

"Why not?"

"Marsden attacked her and as long as that man poses a danger..."

"Ah." Rush stepped forward again with a sigh. "So it's war with our neighbors, is it? I shouldn't be surprised. We Smiths never stay out of trouble for long."

"We've got a knack for it." Triston nodded. "But I'll do my best. Emma is staying here, but I'll go see her mother. Perhaps she'll make this easy and give her permission."

But if Triston held out any hope, it was dashed an hour later when he sat in front of the viscountess.

"Where is my daughter?"

"In Lady Smith's care," Triston answered, sitting up tall and straight as the viscountess attempted to end his life with just a stare.

"Why would she be there and not here?"

"I think you know why," he answered, knowing that it wasn't the best answer he'd ever concocted but he'd also not pretend at deference.

The viscountess's chin lifted and she continued to glare. "She is being a foolish girl."

"She is not," he answered, his fist tightening in his lap. "Marsden is cruel, and he's been horrific to her. I personally witnessed one event."

The lady sat up then. "Should I force a match, then?"

He stared at her. "That's your solution to a man abusing your daughter? Marrying her to him?"

She glowered back. "You don't understand what's at stake. What we stand to lose if other suitors heard what you're telling me. Or if Marsden defamed her character."

"That's why I'd like to offer my suit instead."

"No," the viscountess fired back. "That is out of the question."

He quirked a brow. "I'm in line for a marquessate."

Her lip curled as she looked at him. "I will not debase either of us by articulating how much more suitable Lord Marsden is."

The ridiculousness of that comment had the simmering anger bubble up from where he'd been hiding it just under the surface. "Suitable? You want a rapist for a son-in-law?"

"How dare you say such a thing in my company?"

But he was already standing. He knew what this meant. Emma would not receive permission from her family, and he'd likely never see her dowry. Fine by him. He'd provide for his wife while he lived and see her cared for after.

He'd find a way to make certain she had all the money needed to last the whole of her life. "You're right. I shall leave now."

"But my daughter," she cried. "You must return her. If you don't, I'll see you tossed into prison."

Why did his relationships always come to this? But this time, he knew Emma would stand next to him. "You'd have your daughter's husband imprisoned?"

He didn't wait for her answer as he strode for the door.

———

ABBY DELIVERED a fresh dressing gown and night rail to Emma, and once she was dressed, a tray of food was brought in as well.

She sat picking at cheese and figs as she waited for Triston to return, but she could hardly eat. Triston was the strongest person she knew and yet her mother was a lioness. She'd take a few bites from Triston if she had the opportunity.

Emma had wanted to go with him, but he'd refused to let her, saying that keeping her away from her mother gave him leverage. She could understand that, considering she never had any when it came to her mother.

But when a horse whinnied outside, she jumped from the bed, sure that Triston had returned. Had he successfully negotiated a match for them? Crossing the room, she stepped up to the window, waving. But her hand instantly dropped again.

Because it was not Triston who stood out on the drive but six men, all in dust-covered coats.

She drew in a breath. Who were they and why were they here? Had they come for her? Some other reason?

Her heart pounded wildly in her chest as she took a step back from the window, afraid to be seen.

The door to the room flew open and she bit back a scream as she spun. It was only Abby who stood in the doorway, holding out a hand. "Come on."

"Where are we going?" she asked, swallowing down her fear as she scurried across the room to take Abby's hand.

"To safety," Abby said, pulling her up the stairs to the third floor, straight down the narrow hall to the end, where Emma noticed a wooden ladder leaning against the wall.

"Here," Abby said and then she picked up the ladder, using it to slide a panel in the ceiling into the attic. They climbed up, and Abby pulled the ladder in with her, replacing the panel once again.

The attic was dark with just a bit of daylight filtering in from a vent at the end, the last bits of sunlight shining through the cracks. Abby crossed to the vent and Emma followed, the two women peeking through it.

Rush stood on the large front porch, his arms crossed as he addressed the men. "State your name and your business here."

"It's not you we want," one of the men in the center of the group called back. "It's the boxer."

Rush pulled a pistol from each hip, holding them both down at his sides. "You have an issue with my brother, you go through me first. Now, as I said, state your name and your business."

"We've been sent by Guiltmore to teach your brother what it means to threaten a man like him."

"Funny," another voice called from down the drive. Emma's gaze lifted to see Triston riding toward them. "But why didn't he teach me himself when last I saw him?"

"Never you mind—"

"You should mind," Triston returned. "Because the answer is that he couldn't. He's not strong enough, and if we're being honest, neither are you."

The crack of a gun firing echoed through her ears and then into her heart as the organ seized in her chest.

Emma hadn't seen the shot being fired because her gaze had been fixed on Triston, but she heard it.

She squeezed her eyes shut as she crouched down, a low moan falling from her lips. Had Triston been hurt?

Several more shots filled the air, acrid smoke filling her nostrils and mouth while Abby held on to her, clinging to each other without speaking.

The sound of grunts, shouts, and the clash of metal was next, the roar of men fighting like the boxing match she'd attended and yet different.

Triston was not just in danger of being hurt, he was in real danger of death. Despite the worry coursing through her, she lifted her head. She had to know if he was all right.

Still holding Abby, she looked through the slats to see Triston in the center of the action, swinging a short sword over his head as men cowered around him. Something in her unwound at the sight.

Her future husband never ceased to prove that his strength could hold up her world.

She gave Abby a squeeze. "It's all right."

"They're still fighting," Abby said against her arm, her voice laced with fear. "And there were so many men—"

She rubbed Abby's back as she held her friend. "Yes, but none of those men were Smiths. Rush and Triston have the situation well in hand."

Abby lifted her head too, peeking out the vent and letting out a long breath. "You're right."

Had Emma worried that Triston wasn't the right choice? As the remaining criminals scurried down the road, the brothers stood shoulder to shoulder, an impenetrable wall between her and Abby and the world beyond.

"They are quite the men," Emma whispered as much to herself as to Abby.

"Rush saved me," Abby said by way of answer. "From a terrible fate. Did I tell you that?"

Emma turned to Abby, her lips parting in surprise. "No."

"My guardian would have destroyed my life. It was Rush who repaired the damage. All of it." She touched Emma's face. "Triston will save you too."

She gave Abby a smile. "I know he will, but thank you for confiding in me."

Rising, Abby held out her hand. "Let's go collect our heroes, shall we? It's time for their reward."

Emma nodded as all that fear was replaced with excitement. A reward—that was exactly what Triston needed from her, and she'd give all that she had to give him what he deserved.

CHAPTER FIFTEEN

TRISTON TURNED BACK to the house, looking strong, he knew he still did, but inside, he'd wilted.

Because while he knew the gaming hells would provide financially for Emma, they'd brought trouble right to the door.

But what else might he do to provide for her? Boxing was a young man's game and not lucrative enough, and the boxing club he'd planned to purchase wouldn't bring in enough money either.

Triston ran a frustrated hand through his hair as his thoughts spun around and around, attempting to think of a solution.

He needed to keep Emma safe, and he needed to provide for her, but what if he couldn't do both?

What if...the only way to keep her safe was to let her go?

Not to Marsden. But some other lord who was financially stable, not involved with criminals and illegal activities. The other man would give Emma the life she deserved.

He'd no more made it back into the house than the very subject of his thoughts came racing toward him, her bare feet slapping across the floor as she lifted the hem of her night rail.

He caught her up in his arms, burying his face into her silky hair as he held her to his chest. Tris squeezed his eyes shut and breathed her in.

"Oh, Tris. That was…"

"I know," he answered as he carried her up the stairs away from Rush and Abby. They had to talk, and some privacy was in order.

"I'm so glad you weren't hurt," she whispered in his ear, her fingertips skating over his neck.

Blast, but he loved her touch. The warmth and intimacy of it. Her hands on him had somehow calmed the beast, giving him new direction and purpose and he'd miss… "I'm fine," he answered gruffly, entering his room and kicking the door closed.

"What's wrong?" she asked, her brow furrowing as she pulled back to search his face.

"You could have been hurt," he answered, his voice rough with his worry.

But that made her face soften and she gave him one of those sweet smiles that always managed to leave him hectic inside. "I was safe with you."

He set her down then, keeping his arms around her. "Were you?"

"What?" Her brows drew together, and she studied him as her hands rested on his shoulders. "I am never safer than when I am with you."

He shook his head. "Emma." He hated the words he was about to say but he forced them through his lips. He was never one to shy away from unpleasantness. "You'd be safer with someone else. My life is full of trouble, which came straight at you today."

"No," she protested, shaking her head. "Not straight at me. You were between me and what happened today."

He let out a long-frustrated breath. "Yes, but what if I wasn't? What if you'd been here alone or what happens when we return to London and are off at the club? I must face the fact that—"

"What?" she asked, her breath catching and tears shimmering in her eyes.

"That…" He reached for her face, feeling the silk of her cheek under his rough hands. "That I'm not good for you."

"But you are."

He dropped his hand. "A few hours ago, you were questioning whether or not being with me was another example of your poor judgment."

"You think I have poor judgment?"

She sounded hurt as she curled away from him. His jaw tightened as he winced with regret. "No."

"Then why don't you trust it now?" She crossed her arms which had the effect of plumping her chest and making him ache all the more.

"It's not you I don't trust, it's the world. It's my place in the world. I'm not above the filth like so many of the peerage, Emma, I'm down wallowing in it. Don't you understand?"

And there it was. Why he hated the shininess of her world. Because it would never be his.

———

EMMA COULD FEEL him closing off, the frown pulling at his face as his features grew hard and distant.

She'd not allow it.

Pulling at the ties on her dressing gown, she let the fabric slip from her shoulders and slide to the ground.

His eyes darkened as he took in the thin white night rail that skimmed down her body. Her first victory.

For too long, she'd allowed others to make decisions for her. With clarity, she could see that part of the reason she always moved in the wrong direction was because she was attempting to pull away from her mother's dictates, her mother's choices.

But not this time. This time, she'd not react. She'd take charge.

Triston was meant to be hers and she'd have her way. Stepping closer, she pulled at the ribbon that held her loose braid together, unthreading the hair so that it fell free over her shoulder.

"Emma," he said, his voice sounding strained. Good.

"You call my life shiny? Clean?" She shook her head. "With my mother clawing for money and sacrificing her daughter's future to obtain it?"

He grimaced. "That is a good point."

She stepped closer then. Not touching him, but close enough that she could feel the heat rolling off him. It was a heat she wanted pressed into her skin.

"And tell me. How am I going to find this other shiny man? Is my mother going to be responsible for procuring him? I think we know how that will go."

"You've a point there too, but—"

She wasn't done. "Will you help me find a more suitable husband? Chaperone our teas? Watch as we leave for carriage rides?"

Before she could even gasp, he reached for her, his hand settling in the small of her back and pulling her to his front. "Hell no," he said, his teeth clenching together. Then he shook his head. "I understand—"

"Do you?" she asked, her hands coming to his chest. "If there is one thing I've learned, Triston, it's that once you start down a path, you can't always return to where you've begun. I'm here. My mother knows I'm here."

"Right," he whispered, wrapping his other arm about her then. "You can't marry another now, can you?"

"Even if I could"—she shook her head—"I wouldn't. My heart is too far gone now, Triston. It belongs with you. There is no going back."

"Your heart?" he said as he slid his hands up her back and then down again, cupping her derriere to pull their hips together. As her soft center pushed into his hard cock, they both sucked in air. "Are you trying to melt mine?"

"I…" She drew in a breath to prepare herself for the next words. Emma had done a lot of useless running away. From her mother, from her feelings, but not any longer. "I love you, Triston, and I know my place is with you. Nowhere else."

"Woman," he growled, dropping his mouth close to hers. "Keep talking like that and you'll never be rid of me."

"Oh good." She started to say more but his mouth claimed hers in the sort of hard kiss that stole her breath. When he finally lifted his head, she felt a bit confused, dazed. "That's the point, I'd say."

"Is it?" His lips brushed over hers again before he lifted her into his arms. "In that case, I love you too. Though I must warn you, my love comes at a steep price."

Excitement sizzled through her. "What price?"

"You're going to be spending a great deal of time in my bed."

CHAPTER SIXTEEN

TRISTON KNEW he'd waded into water well over his head. Metaphorically speaking. Emma, always open and honest, confessing that she was in love with him, had unlocked some next layer in his heart.

The deepest. The one from which he'd never return.

She was fighting for him. To be his. And what was more, she'd won. Complete and total knockout.

Had he ever thought her silly? Foolish? She was brave, and strong, and the most perfect creature to ever—

He stopped thinking as she kissed him, her tongue licking at the seam of his mouth as she cradled the base of his skull in both her hands.

He opened, his tongue thrusting against her with all the passion, longing, and love that had been building in him since he'd first met her. Now was his chance to kiss all that skin he'd been dreaming of.

Placing her on the bed, he pulled away even as she cried out her protest and then lifted up on her elbows. "Where are you going?"

"I'm going to lock the door," he said as he crossed the room, turning the key in the lock. This time, they'd not be interrupted.

"Oh," she said in a rush of air. "I see. Because…"

He turned back to her, drinking in the sight. Her hair was undone, cascading about her. Her breasts were pushed forward, her legs hanging off the side of the bed.

A noise reverberated in his throat, his body clenching at the sight. She was all his. "Sweetheart," he said as he stalked toward her, his eyes never leaving her.

She shrank back the slightest bit, and he slowed his pace, attempting to calm the fire surely burning in his eyes.

He knew he radiated intensity. But she was so gorgeous, and in this moment, for the first time, she was all his.

"Don't be afraid, sweetheart," he said as he stopped at the edge of the bed.

She lay back then, reaching out her arms to him. "I'm not afraid. Just a bit nervous, I suppose."

He didn't need to be inside her today. Honestly, he'd very much like to be, but more than that, he just wished to touch her, hold her, perhaps worship her until she broke apart in his arms. It would be enough for now.

But as he bent down, resting his hands on either side of her, leaning over her, she ran a finger over his mouth. "I'm ready."

"Ready?"

"To be yours." And then her finger trailed along his jaw and around the shell of his ear.

He stood again, shucking his jacket, his cravat, his vest, and his shirt. Next, he kicked off one of his hessians, while Emma began pulling the hem of her night rail up her legs past her knees.

Those calves…he'd never been so aware of shapely legs before, but hers drove him mad. He dropped down to his knees, one boot still on, planting a kiss on the inside of her ankle.

She giggled, sitting up so that she could see him over the edge of the bed. "What are you doing?"

"Something I've been dreaming about," he answered as he started kissing a path up her leg, licking at the spot just behind her knee and then nipping at her delectable thigh.

He could smell the tang of her arousal as her legs spread wider for him and he knew that he was going to taste her.

He took his time, savoring the skin of her thigh over and over until she was squirming under the hand he'd placed on her belly.

With a grin, he slid her night rail even higher and then placed a light kiss right in the center of her womanhood.

She let out a moan that made him groan with satisfaction. He kissed her again, flicking his tongue through her folds, and she bucked against him, her fingers threading into his hair.

A smile curled his lips as he started licking up and down her in a steady rhythm before he focused his attention on her little nub of pleasure.

He felt the tension building in her body as she pulled him closer, her nails scraping against his scalp.

He didn't mind the pain—in fact a man like him, he liked it, it made the experience somehow more real, more satisfying, and he increased the pressure as her heels dug into his back, urging him forward.

She twisted under his touch, her whimpers and cries only pushing him on until finally, he inserted a finger inside her channel. She was so wet and tight that he momentarily forgot himself when she clenched around him, gasping out his name.

Like a vise, she held his finger inside her as she broke apart, crying out as her thighs locked tight about his head.

He roared in satisfaction and then stood, quickly yanking off the other boot, though he likely looked ridiculous, hopping around on one leg as he tugged.

It wasn't even that he needed his finish, but he wanted his skin against hers. To kiss her and hold her.

She lay limp on the bed and once he'd shed his boot, he reached for the hem of her night rail, pulling the fabric up and over her head.

He wanted to see all of her, touch her silken skin. He traced his hands over the flare of her hips, across her flat belly, holding her tiny waist.

She was his. All his.

"Emma," he growled out as she lifted her arms to him again.

"My love." That pet name on her lips settled directly into his heart as lowered his chest to her.

THE PRESS of Tris's skin had the heat and want rising in Emma once again. She'd been satiated a moment before but as he slipped his arms beneath her back, his mouth coming to hers, all she could feel was the rising desire for more of him.

"Triston," she murmured against his mouth, her hands sliding down his bare back. "I want..." She didn't know how to finish. Did she want him to repeat what he'd just done? It had been magical, but she liked the feel of his body pressed to hers.

There was something about such a powerful man covering her that stroked some deep need inside her.

He didn't answer but he seemed to understand. Sliding his lips down her neck, he kissed a path to her breasts, kissing each of them before sucking one of her nipples into his mouth.

She cried out, wanting more as her hands continued to explore his back, tracing the ridges that rippled up and down the taut skin.

"I want to kiss every inch of you," he said as he lifted his head to stare in her eyes, cupping each of her breasts in his hands.

"And what," she asked, her eyes fluttering closed at the feel of his rough hands sliding over her skin, "do I get to do to you?"

He chuckled at that. "Let me kiss you."

"That's it?" she asked, raising her brows.

That made him really laugh and he slid back up her body, his stomach brushing against hers when he claimed her mouth again.

She lost herself in his kiss, the press of his lips, the swirl of his tongue.

Triston was all strength, and she drank him in, loving the feel of his powerful body, his strong mouth.

Her legs came about his waist, wanting more of his skin.

But as her thighs pressed against him, they brushed not his warm hips but his breeches.

She broke away from the kiss, frowning down at his lower half. "I don't like them."

He quirked a brow. "Too tight? Many women find them appealing."

That made her smile. "They look very good on you."

"Really? Your frown says otherwise."

She traced his spine, her fingers dipping beneath the waist of his breeches. "I want your skin."

He quirked the sexiest smile as he pulled away from her. "What the lady wants..."

And then he was up, unbuttoning the falls and then yanking the fabric down his thighs. Emma had seen him without his clothes earlier but now she really looked, drinking in the view of his massive thighs, sprinkled with hair, and higher, to his member, jutting from his body.

For the first time since they'd started, just a bit of fear crept back in because...

"Triston," she said, staring. "It's so..."

One side of his mouth tugged up as he came toward her again. "Don't worry, love. I can assure you it fits just fine."

"Does it?"

"The first time can be a bit painful, but after that, my size will be an asset."

That, she could believe. "Your size has been an asset since the first moment we met."

He lay down on top of her again, gathering her close as the tip of his member slid against her slick folds.

"Has it?" he kissed her neck and then up higher, sucking the lobe of her ear into his mouth.

"So strong," she sighed out, his lips making her tingle with longing. Or was that the way the tip was sliding through her folds?

"I'll use every ounce of my strength to keep you safe, love. I can promise you that."

"I know you will," she said as he slid inside her the smallest amount. She felt the stretch, a bit of a burn, but also a fullness that left her…satisfied. She turned her face to his, kissing his lips. "Make me yours, Triston."

He cupped her cheek, kissing her again. "Fast or slow?"

"Quick," she answered, drawing in a deep breath. He was always strong and brave. Now she'd be the same.

He thrust inside her, and her body tensed, pain lancing through her.

He stilled, holding her close and softly kissing her as he murmured sweet words of encouragement in her ear.

Slowly, she relaxed and after several minutes, he eased out of her, pushing back in a languid stroke that only twinged, didn't hurt.

A few more and the pain was gone. He kept his movements light, but she could feel the tension drawing his muscles taut as he held back. She remembered the abandon that had come from her own finish, and she knew that he kept his in check, not wanting to hurt her.

"My love," she whispered close to his ear, her arms wrapped about his neck. "I'm ready for all of you now."

He didn't answer but with one more powerful thrust into her, he came undone. She felt his muscles convulse and she held him close as he finished. And then he collapsed on top of her, burying his face into her neck.

"Triston?" she asked as he rolled to the side, pulling her with him.

"Yes, love?" He pulled the covers out from under them and then rearranged them before joining her.

Then, tucking them both in, he held her tight.

"You're my forever." She sighed against his chest as she snuggled in.

His hand spread out on the small of her back. "Try to get rid of me." He kissed the top of her head.

She was half asleep as she smiled. He was a man who took his commitments seriously. Was she counted among them? She was lucky indeed.

CHAPTER SEVENTEEN

TRISTON WOKE to a soft knocking on the door.

It was dark but he had no idea how long he'd been asleep. "What?" he called out, his voice garbled as Emma stirred against his side.

That fully woke him. The soft silk of her skin slid against him as she settled herself closer to his body, her leg coming up about his waist.

"We need to talk," Rush said from the other side of the door.

He let out a long breath, not wanting to leave the bed or the woman who occupied it.

He slid out from under her, anyway, tucking the covers about her as he rose and crossed the room to slide the door open a crack. "What's wrong?"

"Viscount Northville is here."

"Emma's uncle?" he grunted, tension filling his limbs. Had he come to collect his niece? Kill Triston?

"That's the only Viscount Northville I know."

"Now?" he asked again, scrubbing his face.

"Now." Rush shook his head. "He's having tea with Abby."

"Tea?" It was ridiculous to keep asking questions, but that somehow seemed significantly civilized.

"He has humbly requested a word with you," Rush said, raising his brows.

Triston gave a stiff nod. He wasn't the sort of man who ran from conflict. And so, closing the door, he quickly bathed in the now-frigid water left in the bathtub before beginning to dress.

"What do you think he wants?" Emma asked from the bed. She'd clearly woken and was now sitting up, the covers tucked under her arms.

Likely, Northville was here to either negotiate with Triston or kill him, but he'd not share that with Emma. "Just to talk, sweetheart."

She nipped at her lip. "What if that isn't why he's here?"

Half dressed, he returned to the bed and kissed her cheek. "I promise you, I'll be fine. My brother is here, and your uncle is alone. There is no need to worry."

Which wasn't completely true. It was one thing to fight a group of thugs but another to injure a viscount. Even Triston respected that societal rule.

Which was why his chest was tight as a drum as he made his way down the stairs to the front parlor—where he found Lord Northville laughing amicably with Abby while she poured him more tea.

Triston didn't bother with niceties upon entering the room. "Are you sure you wouldn't prefer something stronger?"

Northville raised a single brow. "Perhaps after our negotiation."

That last words made some of the tension in Tris ease. "Very well."

"I should like a scotch before I return to Minerva. Emma's mother. She's going to be furious."

Triston smiled at that, fully relaxing. "She is a woman who likes to get her way."

"She's worse than a cat and her claws are much sharper. How my brother—" Northville stopped. "You're marrying my niece."

It wasn't a question, but he answered like it was. "Yes."

"And her dowry?"

"I don't need it." He stood up straighter, not even having sat yet. "I'll support Emma myself and make certain her future is provided for."

"Oh, I know you will. You've got the most lucrative club in all of London," her uncle answered. "And you've made inquiries into purchasing a second."

"How did you—"

He held up his hand. "It doesn't matter. What does matter is that it is not Lady Northville's right to negotiate Emma's marriage, it's mine."

"I see." Triston sat then, the turn of events sincerely catching him off guard.

"Are you buying the Den of Sins on your own or with your brothers?"

He looked over at Rush, who shook his head, raising up his hands in question. "To be determined," he answered.

Northville held his gaze with a level stare. "I'll front your family the money, with Emma's dowry, you'll be able to finance any repairs and startup costs."

Triston started to protest but Northville held up a hand. "You'll replace it...quickly. And you'll reimburse me, giving me a higher percentage for backing you."

Triston looked at Rush again, who gave a quick jerk of his chin to agree. Neither of them had wished to be in the gaming business, but as Rush's arm slipped about Abby, Triston knew that his brother had made the same decision as Tris. Caring for his wife came before anything else.

"Done," he said without hesitation.

"Now," Northville said, looking at Abby, who seemed to understand exactly what he wished. Silently, she crossed to the tray with the whiskey, pouring three glasses. "In terms of your enemy."

"You're going to have to explain."

"My dear," he said to Abby as she handed him a glass, "would you give us a moment, please?"

"Of course," Abby said with a smile, handing him and Rush their drinks before she left the room. Tris noted that she left the door open.

But Northville didn't seem to mind.

Northville drew in a deep breath. "I am a second son. A spare. My father bought me a military commission and I served for several years before returning to join society. Only I was actually still part of an elite group of service members focused on the Eastern threat."

"Eastern threat?" Rush asked, pushing off the mantel and coming to sit next to Triston. "What Eastern threat?"

But a niggle of fear had started in Triston's chest and he stared at the other man, half understanding the truth already.

"Count Gyla."

Gyla. The name of Guiltmore's boss. "He's a count?"

"Who's a count?"

"Gyla is the man behind Guiltmore, who has been trying to buy our club."

Northville sat forward. "He's purchased five already, knocking any opposition flat. That is until he reached the Smiths." Northville gave him a small smile and then took a sip of his whiskey. "You have not only managed to hold him off, but you also took a club back. Most impressive."

"We weren't really responsible for the return of the Den of Sins."

"Your partners were, though, and that tells me a few things. You're smart. You know how to align yourselves, and you'll make an excellent protector for my sometimes-wayward niece." Northville raised his glass. "And an excellent partner for me."

"Thank you," Triston said, raising his glass as well, though all he had just learned still swirled in his thoughts.

"The government is aware of Gyla and is actively working on removing him from the country. Your job is only to hold him off long enough for the crown to see him gone."

That made Triston feel slightly better. A temporary threat that he only had to keep at bay for a short time. "Good."

"Excellent." Northville rose, holding out his hand.

Triston did the same, rising from his seat and clasping the viscount's hand in his. "Welcome to the family."

Triston gave a quick jerk of his chin in acknowledgment. This was not at all what he'd expected from this meeting. But as he returned to his seat and took another swallow of his whiskey, he couldn't help but feel that fate had intervened.

Emma would be his forever.

Smiling, he let Rush talk with the viscount. This was exactly where he was meant to be.

EPILOGUE

ONE MONTH LATER...

A FEW SNOWFLAKES dotted the air as Emma stepped from the carriage in front of the small chapel in the village.

Her family waited, as did a few members of the Smith clan. Gris and Fulton had remained in London and Ace had stayed in Northern England, where he was attempting to repair his derelict estate.

Emma did not give a fig who else was in attendance, provided she married Triston today.

She'd never been readier for anything.

Her mother was grudgingly in attendance as well. Emma assumed her uncle had insisted. Nat was here too, and she was preparing for her season in London just a few short months away.

Her uncle would allow her mother and sister to stay with him, escorting them both to ensure that Nat made the best match possible.

Emma knew whomever her sister married would be wonderful. Nat deserved the best, and she seemed thrilled that despite the odds, Emma had found her soulmate.

Today was Emma's day. She drew in a deep breath of air as her uncle greeted her, offering her his elbow. "Ready?"

"Ready," she answered, glowing with happiness as she floated through the church doors.

Triston stood at the front, Rush by his side. Their eyes met and locked, and she moved toward him, his gaze like a beacon home.

When she slid her fingers into his, a sigh escaped her lips. This was where she belonged.

The words of the ceremony washed over her, while the candles flickered about them.

And when their lips met, Emma smiled against his mouth, so filled with joy she could hardly contain it.

As he lifted his head, his brows rising, she gave out the smallest whoop and exclaimed, "We did it!"

The church was filled with quiet laughter as Triston's arm slipped about her. "My Emma."

They made their way down the aisle, her feet hardly touching the floor. "I nearly added some lines to the vows about when I am stuck in trees or when I slip into cold rivers…"

He stopped for a moment, not laughing, but looking deadly serious as he said, "I shall always be there to catch you."

She kissed him again, despite everyone watching. Because her heart couldn't wait another moment.

They made their way back to Rush and Abby's home, where a breakfast was laid out for all the guests.

They'd determined to stay at a lovely inn in a nearby village so that they might have some time alone, and then they'd return to London, where they'd take up residence with Fulton and Gris before Triston would find them a home of their own.

Emma was only the slightest bit nervous. She'd never lived with young men before, particularly unmarried ones, but she knew that Triston would find them a home soon enough.

And as the guests left and they loaded into a carriage, any reservations she had slipped away. She was married to Triston.

He settled her on his lap, his lips finding hers as he held her tightly to his chest. The kiss went on and on until she could barely think, the ache in her body was so tight. "Tris," she moaned into his mouth.

He eased his lips away. "Very soon, my love."

Her brow creased as she looked back at him. "It's not fair to tease like that."

He laughed, pulling a few envelopes from his breast pocket. "We've received notes from family who could not attend. Shall we open them?"

She nodded, easing off his lap as he tucked her against his side and then broke the seal open on one of the envelopes. The first was from the Earl of Easton.

Triston scanned the contents and then handed the letter to her.

"What does it say?" She started to read as well and then gasped, looking back a Triston. "A townhouse?"

"In Mayfair." Triston shook his head.

"It's a gift from your half-brother?" Her fingers shook. They'd have a home of their very own.

"Something like that," he said with a smile. "I don't want you to worry about your future. I'll see that you are provided for, Emma."

She gave him a glowing smile. "I have every confidence."

He slid open the second envelope, his brow creasing.

"Triston?"

He stared at the sheet of paper, frowning heavily. "We have to go back."

"What's wrong?"

"It's Gris."

"What's wrong with Gris?" Her heart began to hammer in her chest as worry coursed through her.

"He doesn't say precisely, he just begs one of us to return to London. He's in desperate need of aid. And the final line is a plea for whichever brother answers to bring his wife."

"What?" Emma asked, plucking the paper from Tris's hand, and after reading the letter, she looked up at her husband, completely confused. "Why would he make a plea for me or Abby to come to London?"

"I don't know, and I'm so sorry, love, but we have to go back to Rush and likely to London."

She kissed him again. "I understand. Family is everything. If it were Natalie, I wouldn't even hesitate."

He kissed her back, long and hard and full of the passion she loved so much. Then he knocked on the wall of the carriage, telling the driver to turn around.

"I'll turn in the next village," the driver called back. "Just sit tight, my lord."

"Done," he murmured before he pulled her into his lap again and flicked up the hem of her skirts. "It will take a solid hour until we reach Rush and Abby's."

"So it will." Her stomach fluttered and she gave him a coquettish smile.

"And there is nothing that we can do for Gris in that time."

"No, I suppose there isn't."

With his arm behind her, he nudged her back into a semi-reclined position, pulling the hem of her gown higher. "We may as well fill the time with something."

And then his hand traveled up her thigh…

A BARGAIN with a Beast
By Tammy Andresen

PROLOGUE

THE SUN HAD JUST BEGUN to lighten the sky, when Reynalda Pierce stepped onto King Street. She shivered in the cold and pulled her shawl tighter, hitching the basket that she carried higher on her arm.

No good deeds were ever done at this hour.

She knew the street well enough, having come to this part of Cheapside to see a client a year before. He'd paid highly enough that she hadn't needed to work for a solid month. Which was a detail of note, unfortunately for him.

Because the time lapse had been just long enough for her to realize, a month later, that she carried his child. She'd come back to this street half a dozen times to tell him so, but she'd lost her nerve every time and returned to her tiny room on the East End of London without a word to the man who'd fathered her daughter.

She knew it was wrong, not telling him, but she'd also been acquainted with enough men to know that they didn't always take kindly to unwanted children. So she'd determined to raise the child on her own. An ill-fated plan to say the least.

The baby had come, a perfect little girl with ten tiny fingers and ten sweet toes, sleepy eyes, and a shock of black hair that looked just like her papa's. Reynalda remembered that about him. The dark hair and eyes, and a powerful body that despite his strength, hadn't been harsh or cruel. In fact, he'd been surprisingly gentle, kind even despite his rough exterior.

Worries aside, she knew she made the right choice this cold morning in December despite the fog that cast its eerie shadow on London.

She wrapped the blankets tighter about her perfect Rose and tucked her deeper into the basket. "Your papa is a good man, I think," she whispered to the drowsy child. "Healthy and strong, not like your mama." Two tears slid down Reynalda's face as she stared down at the innocent face of her daughter. "I've left a note for you explaining that I love you, my sweet girl. Grow up big and strong. You have a bright future ahead."

Rose didn't make a peep at Reynalda's plea, the tightly swaddled blankets having lulled the baby into sleep. The night's chill still hung in the December air. Christmastide was coming.

But Rose would be warm enough. Reynalda had used every last blanket she possessed to wrap the baby in warmth. Pulling her shawl even tighter about her own shoulders, Reynalda suppressed the cough that beat in her chest. It would do no good to be discovered now.

She hated to leave Rose, but she couldn't stay. She had no future to offer her beautiful daughter, and so with one last glance at her perfect little face, Reynalda turned and slipped down the street in the dark, saying a prayer for her sweet baby girl....

A BARGAIN WITH A BEAST

Gris woke to a familiar sound, his brother Fulton cursing like a sailor. "What the ever-loving fucking Christ is this fucking doing—"

Gris rolled over to return to sleep, unconcerned by the litany of profanity. The language was expected. Fulton was a sailor, after all. Technically, he was a smuggler who sailed regularly to pick up product, but he spent most of his time around criminals, gamblers, or seamen and so his mouth was foul. To be fair, Gris's wasn't much better.

"Gris," his brother roared, likely from the bottom of the stairs. "Get your lazy fucking ass—"

Fulton was cut off by a mournful wail that made Gris bolt into the sitting position in his bed. "What was that?"

Fulton didn't answer. Instead, the crying continued, punctuated by the thunderous falls of Fulton's feet stomping up the stairs.

A moment later the door burst open, crashing into the wall. Fulton stood in the hall, feet planted wide and a murderous expression on his face. His hands were in front of his body, held out as far from his person as they might reach, a basket dangling from his closed fist.

Gris jumped from the bed, shirtless, and still a bit dazed from sleep. "Fulton?"

In answer, Fulton strode into the room, his nostrils flared, and his lip curled. "Special delivery for you." Fulton's tone held a note of worry that Gris had never heard before. Alarming, considering the amount of trouble in which the other Smith regularly found himself.

"What's for me? What delivery? I'm not expecting anything…" He looked down at the basket, his mind grappling with the noise he heard. A goat? Kittens? For a second, he scrubbed his face, trying to think but his brain was so muddled, it just didn't work. He'd taken the earlier shift of the gaming hell they owned and operated and then he'd come home and gotten good and drunk.

He was not exactly certain why he'd overindulged. Perhaps because it was Tuesday? Or was it Wednesday? Whatever the day, he couldn't quite calm the restless feeling that had been rising in him like the tide.

He liked the club just fine, liked his side business of making gin for the club. It had a precision that the rest of his life lacked, and he found it…soothing. It had been his escape for most of his adult life.

Until a few months prior, his entire family had lived in their townhouse, five brothers and two sisters. But now, several of his siblings had married and most had moved away to the four corners of England. And now that they were gone, if he were being completely honest, he missed them.

Especially his sisters Mirabelle and Anna. Mirabelle had married but Anna had just travelled off with his eldest brother to be safe. Their gaming hell had brought as much trouble as it had money.

The trouble he could handle, but the threat to his family, that was a problem that needed solving. Quickly. Not that he'd made a hell of a lot of progress, but he was trying.

His father, the Earl of Easton, likely would have told Gris that, as usual, he wasn't trying hard enough. He scrubbed his face, attempting to focus on the present. He and his siblings were the bastard children of the Earl of Easton, and the world was a cold hard place for children born out of wedlock. For all children, really.

"Are you listening?" Fulton barked.

Had his brother been talking? "What time is it?"

A BARGAIN WITH A BEASTgment>

"I don't know. Six."

"In the morning?" No wonder his mind wasn't working. He'd likely only been asleep for an a few hours and he'd had an excessive amount of gin.

"Yes, in the morning," Fulton spit, holding the basket up higher. "What does it matter what time it is?"

"Because…" But he stopped talking as first his gaze caught the letter that was pinned to the side of the basket. In very neat scroll was written his name….

Lord Griswold Smith

And then he looked in the basket and the source of the noise became clear. In the folds of the blankets was a squalling baby, its face screwed up and wrinkled as shrieks sounded from its lips.

"What the—"

"My thoughts exactly," Fulton said with a nod and then set the basket on the floor, turning toward the door.

"Where are you going?" he yelled at his brother, panic rising in him at the idea of being left with the squalling baby. He'd helped care for his sisters but that had been when both girls were older. Mira was only a few years younger than him and Anna only five years his junior.

"I'm leaving," Fulton said over his shoulder. "That thing is addressed to you."

He stepped around the basket, chasing after his brother. "Fulton. You can't leave. What the hell am I supposed to do with it?"

Fulton spun, his massive shoulders barely fitting in the doorframe as he ran a hand through his dark hair. "How am I supposed to know? They don't teach baby care on ships or in gaming hells."

Gris looked back at the basket, and widened his eyes as the keen of the cry rose to a new, more ear-piercing pitch.

More boots sounded on the steps and their cook appeared behind Fulton. "What on God's green earth is making that racket?"

Relief at the sight of the crotchety old woman made Gris's shoul-

125

ders slump with relief. Surely Mrs. Mable, the cook, knew how to make a baby stop crying. "Missus Mable I'm going to need—"

She raised a finger silencing him. "I don't take care of babies."

"But—" He held out his hands. "It's crying."

"Where did it come from?" she asked, scowling at the basket as she continued to hide behind Fulton.

"Found it on the front stoop when I came in from my late shift at Hell's Corner. It's got a note with Gris's name on it."

Mrs. Mable stretched up even further to look over Fulton's shoulder. "So it does."

Gris turned back to look at the wailing child. "It's not mine."

"How do you know," Fulton reasoned, cocking his head to the side. "Perhaps you should look at the letter."

He didn't want to. Reading that letter seemed a bit like claiming the child, but he found himself crouching down and plucking the paper from the pin.

And with each word he read, his head pounded a bit more. Rose. That was her name. Without thinking, he lay a hand on the baby's chest, giving her an awkward pat to attempt to soothe the little thing. The crying was near splitting his head in two.

Immediately, tiny hands emerged from the blankets, each wrapping about one of his fingers as it pulled his hand toward her mouth. He dropped the letter as the crying instantly stopped a mouth opening wide as it stuck his middle finger into her little mouth and began to suck.

His eyes widened at the pressure. "Strong little thing."

"It's crying because it's hungry," Mrs. Mable said with a nod. "There is a woman who lives next door to me down on Fletcher Street that just lost a wee one. I bet she'd wet nurse for you."

"Wet nurse?" They were talking about hiring help now? This baby didn't even belong here no matter what that note said. "Why would I hire a wet nurse for some stranger's baby?"

"Going to let it starve?" Fulton asked, with a crease to his brow.

"You could leave it out on the stoop." Mrs. Mable added. "It's a regular occurrence where I'm from."

His lip curled in distaste. "Surely there is someplace we can take the baby. Someone will care for her."

"I doubt it," Mrs. Mable said. "Or else why would so many people just leave them to die of exposure?"

Was that pitch of his stomach the gin or did it offend him to think of people doing such a thing to a defenseless little creature?

Not that he wanted to keep it. He needed to find this baby's mother. Return the child to her caring arms. But until then... "Contact the wet nurse," he said, reaching into the basket and pulling the baby from the blankets as he awkwardly brought the little thing to his chest.

She nuzzled down into him in the sweetest way, her silky cheek brushing his much rougher skin. Rose cooed as she curled into him unlike any touch he'd ever known. The only other comparable embrace had been from one of his sister's cats.

"Fulton, can you bring me paper and the inkwell?"

"Who are you going to write?" he asked, moving closer, clearly more interested in having his curiosity satisfied about the baby than he was completing the requested task.

"Write to our brothers. They're all married. And we have two sisters. One of the women will know what to do."

Fulton nodded. "That's right. If we're going to be saddled with all these women, they might as well be of use."

Mrs. Mable's hand came out, rapping the back of Fulton's head. No woman had ever treated Fulton so coarsely, but she was magic in the kitchen and apparently, Fulton would allow all sorts of abuse for kidney pie.

"How do you even know the babe is or isn't yours?" Mrs. Mable asked as the baby took a fistful of his chest hair and gave it a hard yank.

He looked at the letter again, knowing he needed to finish it. But the first lines were already burned into his brain.

You might not remember me, Lord Griswold. I was only here the once, a year ago. But you've irrevocably changed my life and our little Rose can't be undone. I can't care for her. Not the way she deserves and so I apologize, but I'm irrevocably changing your life now. I hope you will understand why I didn't tell you sooner. It's not an easy thing to share, especially when you're a woman like me.

Yes. He'd read the rest of this woman's letter later. After he'd solved the baby crisis. Had he been missing his family? He took it back. Now he just wanted his gin and his gaming hell.

But as Rose cooed softly in his arms, her mouth searching his chest, he had a feeling that his life was never going to be the same again.

Want to read more? A Bargain with a Beast can be found on Amazon!

Wish to go back to the beginning of this series?
A Bet with a Baron
A Romp with a Rogue

More Lords of Temptation coming soon!

Keep up with all the latest news, sales, freebies, and releases by joining my newsletter!

www.tammyandresen.com

Hugs!

ABOUT THE AUTHOR

Tammy Andresen lives with her husband and three children just outside of Boston, Massachusetts. She grew up on the Seacoast of Maine, where she spent countless days dreaming up stories in blueberry fields and among the scrub pines that line the coast. Her mother loved to spin a yarn and Tammy filled many hours listening to her mother retell the classics. It was inevitable that at the age of eighteen, she headed off to Simmons College, where she studied English literature and education. She never left Massachusetts but some of her heart still resides in Maine and her family visits often.

Find out more about Tammy:
http://www.tammyandresen.com/
https://www.facebook.com/authortammyandresen
https://twitter.com/TammyAndresen
https://www.pinterest.com/tammy_andresen/
https://plus.google.com/+TammyAndresen/

OTHER TITLES BY TAMMY

Lords of Scandal

Duke of Daring

Marquess of Malice

Earl of Exile

Viscount of Vice

Baron of Bad

Earl of Sin

——————————

Earl of Gold

Earl of Baxter

Duke of Decandence

Marquess of Menace

Duke of Dishonor

Baron of Blasphemy

Viscount of Vanity

Earl of Infamy

Laird of Longing

——————————

Duke of Chance

Marquess of Diamonds

Queen of Hearts

Baron of Clubs

Earl of Spades

King of Thieves

Marquess of Fortune

Calling All Rakes

Wanted: An Earl for Hire

Needed: A Dishonorable Duke

Found: Bare with a Baron

Vacancy: Viscount Required

Lost: The Love of a Lord

Missing: An Elusive Marquess

Wanted: Title of Countess

The Dark Duke's Legacy

Her Wicked White

Her Willful White

His Wallflower White

Her Wanton White

Her Wild White

His White Wager

Her White Wedding

The Rake's Ruin

When only an Indecent Duke Will Do

How to Catch an Elusive Earl

Where to Woo a Bawdy Baron

When a Marauding Marquess is Best

What a Vulgar Viscount Needs

Who Wants a Brawling Baron

When to Dare a Dishonorable Duke

The Wicked Wallflowers

Earl of Dryden

Too Wicked to Woo

Too Wicked to Wed

Too Wicked to Want

How to Reform a Rake

Don't Tell a Duke You Love Him

Meddle in a Marquess's Affairs

Never Trust an Errant Earl

Never Kiss an Earl at Midnight

Make a Viscount Beg

Wicked Lords of London

Earl of Sussex

My Duke's Seduction

My Duke's Deception

My Earl's Entrapment

My Duke's Desire

My Wicked Earl

Brethren of Stone

The Duke's Scottish Lass

Scottish Devil

Wicked Laird

Kilted Sin

Rogue Scot

The Fate of a Highland Rake

A Laird to Love

Christmastide with my Captain

My Enemy, My Earl

Heart of a Highlander

A Scot's Surrender

A Laird's Seduction

Taming the Duke's Heart

Taming a Duke's Reckless Heart

Taming a Duke's Wild Rose

Taming a Laird's Wild Lady

Taming a Rake into a Lord

Taming a Savage Gentleman

Taming a Rogue Earl

Fairfield Fairy Tales

Stealing a Lady's Heart

Hunting for a Lady's Heart

Entrapping a Lord's Love: Coming in February of 2018

American Historical Romance

Lily in Bloom

Midnight Magic

The Golden Rules of Love

Boxsets!!

Taming the Duke's Heart Books 1-3

American Brides

A Laird to Love

Wicked Lords of London

Printed in Great Britain
by Amazon

20264711R00081